MARRIED MEN ON THE LOOSE

First Edition

Published by The Nazca Plains Corporation
Las Vegas, Nevada
2010

ISBN: 9781-61098-007-4
E-book: 978-1-61098-008-1

Published by

The Nazca Plains Corporation ®
4640 Paradise Rd, Suite 141
Las Vegas NV 89109-8000

PUBLISHER'S NOTE
Married Men on the Loose is a work of fiction created wholly by *Wade Wright's* imagination. All characters are fictional and any resemblance to any persons living or deceased is purely by accident. No portion of this book reflects any real person or events.

Wedding Band Image, Slobo
Art Director, Blake Stephens

DEDICATION

To each and every man that has experienced the realization that perhaps, just perhaps, he was living the wrong type of life, and now, the time for some change has come. To each, we wish you the best of luck.

MARRIED MEN ON THE LOOSE

First Edition

Wade Wright

CONTENTS

TYLER, BACHELOR FOR A DAY!

THE VEGAS THING

INTER-RELATIONSHIP TRAINING MEETING

ABOUT THE AUTHOR

TYLER, BACHELOR FOR A DAY!

Chapter One:
I'm All Alone

Tyler was not greatly happy that he was home alone on a nice and bright Sunday morning, with nobody to talk to, nor anybody to neither fix, for him, nor have breakfast with him. His wife had wanted to go visit her Mom and Dad over in Dallas for a few days, and Tyler just simply could not take the time off of work to make the trip. So it was now the Sunday morning that he had been regretting ever since she and the two kids, a son aged six and a daughter, aged eight, drove out of the drive on Thursday morning.

Tyler was not a loner type of a person. At age 32 he was very active in some neighborhood sports groups, and was also pretty active in a city wide Neighborhood Improvement Program, which worked with different neighborhoods in giving them help to clean up an area, or do some other type of work that needed volunteers to help out. Tyler worked in construction, and since he owned and drove a truck, his time and his truck became very beneficial to that group when they needed something hauled away in a pick-up.

It was 7:30 on this Sunday morning as Tyler woke up to find that the sun was out and shinning bright. There was a nice breeze blowing through the house, and fortunately the newspaper driver had done a little better in aiming the newspaper a little more toward the house this time, than the usual – bush area. He remembered with fondness the "old days," as he referred to them, when the newspaper was actually delivered by a boy on a bike, and if you needed to, you could talk to him and ask special favors. Now he did not even know who delivers the paper. He never sees them since they fly by in a car and toss the paper out of the window. As he stepped outside, stood in the warm sun for a moment, picked up the paper, he remembered back the many Sundays that he had thrown a newspaper at this very house, when he was the local newspaper boy.

With the warm sun hitting his bare chest, Tyler stood there for a moment, stared at the fresh flowers that were just starting to bloom and reflected a little of life. Grade school, high school, away for a short time to go to trade school, then back home again to find Jeanny, the love of his life, get married, settle down, have the two kids and finally buy one of the old stable houses, that he had thrown so many newspapers at during his youth. Tyler decided that life was pretty good. On this particular day, pretty lonely, since he was home all alone, but still pretty good!

Turning the paper over and looking at the front page, Tyler quickly decided that "Section A," "Section B" and "Section C" could all be tossed aside, since he felt no need to read about the world's problems, the state's problems, nor the city's problems. He simply was not in the mood to read "downer" stuff! Comics, yes! He drank a re-heated cup of coffee – left over from Saturday morning – once he found the comics and the sports sections. He smiled at the comics, and then frowned at finding out that his favorite High School soccer team, the "Mad Dogs," had lost out in their attempt of moving on to the regional semi-finals.

"Bummer!" Tyler thought! "Damn I was really hoping they could do better this year! Well, that's life! Life! Yeah life – my life! I've got a life to live today, and I'm hungry. Food, yeah, breakfast! Right, me cook? Don't think so!" Tyler was great if it was on the backyard grill, but in the kitchen, he knew – hey – that was one of Jeanny's great qualities.

Being smart enough to know his cooking qualifications, Tyler decided that a nice Sunday morning drive over to Hillsburg, and a visit to the old, and rather famous, Mamma's Kitchen Cafe, and have some of her whole-wheat pancakes, was the order of the day.

Quickly Tyler ran upstairs, showered, and dressed in some rather attractive active sportswear. Since it was Sunday, he did not want to look too sloppy, but at the same time, not as if he had just come from church, either. "Neat, not pretty!" He told himself.

After a quick phone call to Dallas, checking in to make sure everything was "A-OK" there, and getting a chance to tell each of the kids that their Daddy loves them, he headed out the door for his drive over to Hillsburg.

Hillsburg was about a 30 or 35 minute drive across some back roads. Living in a larger town, and having just about everything handy and available there that a person needs, it takes a special day, such as this one, to remind a person that some of the great spots are off of the main roads, and kind of tucked back in. Mamma's Kitchen Cafe was definitely one of them!

Being alone for the week was starting to be of little concern to Tyler now that he had decided how to start his day. He was having the chance to drive a little slower on these back roads, than the normal highway speed, and he was having an unexpected opportunity to just calmly look at the new vegetation that was now coming up with the warmer weather that they had been getting during the past couple of weeks. He was feeling a little more carefree than he had for some time, now. Not a single guy – by any stretch of the imagination – but yet, for a day, he had the opportunity to do as he felt, and if, and when, he felt. Smiling to himself, he actually realized that maybe this "free" day was going to be good for him. No responsibilities, just live life as it happens! Today he knew he was just going to be a bachelor for a day, and let life happen, as it happens!

Having not been in Hillsburg for quite some time, Tyler was very pleased to see that the main street had been completely re-surfaced and looked much "sharper" to him than it had looked before. He pulled his pick-up into the parking lot of Mamma's Kitchen Cafe and took one of the two last parking spots available.

"Wow!" He thought. "This place must still be as good as it was when I was a little shit!" Opening the door, he was greeted by an attractive young high school girl, and offered a seat in the first booth.

"Right here?" She offered, as if asking if he wanted it. It was the first booth right inside of the front door, and he assumed that most people turn it down if they can sit someplace else. Looking around quickly, seeing that it was the last table open, he quickly told the young lady that, "This will be fine!" The young lady handed Tyler a menu, and asked that he have a good meal.

Tyler sat down and a waitress quickly brought him a large glass of water and some table service. "I'll be right back to get your order," the waitress said as she quickly turned to actually run toward the kitchen. Tyler knew that she was probably trying to handle much more work load than any normal person should have to do. The place was packed.

Whole-wheat pancakes, two eggs, bacon, orange juice and coffee was Breakfast Number Two on the menu, and Tyler was almost ecstatic that the whole-wheat pancakes were still there! Reading the menu took only a moment since Number Two was still there and was still being served. As he laid the menu down, he looked up and glanced around his room. "Nice looking place," he thought to himself. "They keep it looking good!" Being in construction, Tyler has a constant eye for how buildings look and what condition they are in. And it is a good "time spender" when he has nothing else to think about at that time. As he was looking around, he could hear the hostess behind him telling a person that the only place available right then was at the counter. Tyler was already feeling rather uncomfortable since he, alone, was seated at a four top, and no other tables were available. He turned to look back as far as he could, and he could see that it was a single man that was standing to the side, waiting for a table, since he had told the waitress that he preferred not sitting at the counter.

Tyler turned to the man and said, "Uh Sir! I'm all alone here at this table. If you don't mind sharing a table with me, you certainly are welcome to join me. I have not even ordered yet."

The man looked at Tyler, and accepted his gracious offer with a smile. "Thank you! I really do appreciate this!" The man said, as he sat down across from Tyler. "Really, I do appreciate this! I was over in Europe a few years ago, and to share tables over there is very common, which I like, but over here, we just don't. So I really do appreciate it!" Then extending his hand forward, to offer a handshake, he continued, "I'm Zack."

Tyler extended his hand, shook hands and told the man that he was Tyler.

The waitress approached the table and acted quite confused, now that there were two men at the table, and she thought there was only the one. Tyler quickly explained to her about how the additional person had not originally been there, but how he had offered the man a seat. Once again acting very confused, she hurried off and grabbed another glass of water and some table service. The two men grinned at each other as she returned with the service, then started to ask for their orders, then decided that since the new guy had just gotten there, maybe they were not ready to order, then she realized that the menu had been there, and then she wondered if they were ready, and she was just all flustered and beside herself!

"Calm down miss." Tyler encouraged her. "Take a deep breath! Stop for a moment. You are getting yourself all confused here. Take a deep breath." He then checked with Zack to see if he was ready to order, and finding out that he was, he then told the waitress that they were ready to order, if she was.

After they ordered, and they rather made sure the waitress had written down what they wanted, she left the table and the two men laughed heartily about her state of confusion. "I just hope we get something close to what we ordered," Zack said, to which Tyler agreed. This rather odd exchange with the waitress certainly did break the ice for Zack and Tyler to enjoy some good conversation and some enjoyable time together.

As they ate, which was what they had ordered, the two men shared a lot of conversation about their personal lives, their schooling, their employment's, and to Zack's special interest Tyler's volunteer work with the neighborhood committee.

Tyler and Zack were rather hitting it off together quite well, and when Zack explained to Tyler that his reason for wanting to know more about the cleanup committee stuff was, that he was thinking about maybe trying to get something like that organized there in Hillsburg since he, right then, had some stuff that needed to be cleaned up, but since he did not have any way of hauling stuff, the cleanup was not getting done.

"Zack, let's go do it! Hey man, I've got all day, all to myself, and if I can help you out some, let's go do it. Can you do it today?" Tyler asked.

"Well yeah, Tyler, I can, but I'm not asking you to help me. That's not fair! Tyler, that's not why I was asking how you guys did that! Beside, look at you. You aren't dressed for doing dirty work like that! Tyler, I can't ask you to do that!"

"OK, listen Zack. You are not asking. I'm telling you that if you have the time today, I want to do it. Hey man, you and I are almost the same size, and I'm sure you've got some old work clothes hanging around somewhere that I can borrow long enough to do that. Right?"

"Well, yeah, right. Yes, I do have some clothes that you can borrow, but I still feel funny about you helping me do this. Are you sure?"

"Zack, if I didn't want to do it, I'm smart enough to not say that I wanted to. OK?"

"OK then, if you say so!"

The two made plans that Tyler would follow Zack to his house, after – to Zack's insistence – he would pay for the meals.

As the two vehicles approached Zack's house, Tyler could agree that some cleaning up really did need to take place. Zack's house sat back quite a long lane. It was not actually in the town of Hillsburg, but was one of the first "country" places right outside of town. Not the big kind of a place often referred to as a "country place," but a piece of property that did not have another house right up close beside it.

The two parked and Zack told Tyler to follow him into the house. Tyler found the interior of the house to be very attractive, and not really anything like the exterior. The exterior displayed the fact that this was a much older piece of property, although well taken care of, but none the less, an older house. The inside had been completely re-done, and could have easily come from the pictures of the larger New York City loft apartments.

"Nice, nice!" Tyler stammered as he looked around. "Zack, what a surprise when a person comes in here from the outside for the first time. This is sharp! I like this!"

"Thanks! I appreciate that. Kevin has done all of it! I don't know if I mentioned that he's an interior designer. And if I say so myself, I think he is damn good."

"I know you mentioned Kevin, but maybe I didn't realize that maybe Kevin is a little more than just a renter —— right?" Tyler asked.

"Tyler, he's my partner. My lover! Tyler, I thought you understood that! No, he's not my business partner, he is my life partner. Oh Tyler, I'm sorry! Tyler I did not mean to hide the fact that we are lovers. Oh Tyler, I'm sorry!"

"Hey don't get upset Zack. Right, I did not understand, but that's my fault, not yours. No big deal, well-unless my being here with you while he is not here is a problem. Is my being here going to cause any problem?"

"God no, Tyler! Us gay guys are like straight people. We interact with others like, should I say, normal people do! We interact with more than just our partners."

"Where is Kevin? Do I get to meet him?"

"He's at a convention in New York City this week. That's why I was down at Mamma's Kitchen Cafe for breakfast this morning. If I'm by myself, I prefer going someplace to eat than to fix something here and eat by myself."

In the confusion of Tyler not completely understanding the relationship between Zack and Kevin, they managed to compare their confusion with the total confusion the waitress had earlier. That made the two laugh at the mistake.

The confusion did offer the opportunity for the two men to have an open conversation about life styles and actions in living. The conversation did actually get around to Zack, quite openly, asking Tyler if he had ever played with another guy.

"God Zack, you are really making me go back in my history now. Yeah! Once! I was in St. Louis at trade school, and one of the classmates and I got real drunk one night, and we went farther than I'm sure we should have."

"So, tell me, what happened?" Zack quickly asked.

"Well I was what – probably only about 19 or 20 and of course too young to drink. So this guy, his name was Robert, he was already over 21 and he could buy beer and gin. Gin, why gin, I have no idea, but he drank gin. Well anyway, I was over at his place, a small apartment, above a garage, behind a house, and we started drinking his beer. Well pretty soon he had to go buy more beer, and while he was at the corner store, I discovered some gay mags that he had some other stuff on top of. I wasn't snooping on purpose, I just wanted something to read while he was gone. Well, anyway, when he got back, I was sitting there with my mouth hanging wide open looking at some real active pictures. I did not know if he did that stuff or not, and I looked at him and asked. He told me yeah, and that he was gay. Until then, I did not know that. Well, anyway, I had already had a lot to drink, especially for a guy that never gets to drink, and we – well – we kind of started doing some of the stuff that were in the pictures. He kept pouring beer down me so that I'd keep doing his stuff and I finally woke up with one hell of a hangover the next day about two in the afternoon."

"So, do you remember what stuff you guys did?"

"Part of it. Hell he got me so damn drunk, I'm not sure what we did later. Some of it I remember, some of it he told me I did, but I'm not sure. I was too far out of it to actually remember.

"Have you ever thought about doing it again? You said you did it once. Ever think about doing it again?"

"Zack, you are putting me on the spot here man. I don't like lying, and you are a gay guy asking me if I ever thought about having more gay sex. Zack, maybe we had better just change clothes and go get that stuff picked up that we wanted to get done. OK?"

"Yeah Tyler, I'm sorry! I was not trying to put you on the spot. I'm really sorry that I asked! I'm sorry!"

"Hey Zack, no sweat man! We're both big enough and old enough to take care of ourselves. No problem."

"Well I'm sorry I asked. I apologize!"

"Zack, knock it off man! Now, some dirty old clothes of yours that I can put on my nice, straight man, pure, body! What do I get to wear that you haven't washed yet?" Tyler asked with a big grin on his face!"

As Zack was digging through a stack of folded clothes, he heard Tyler's humorous remark, and he replied, "Tyler, don't go there man! Don't play with me – unless you are going to play with me!" He grinned and looked at Tyler.

Zack pulled out some cutoffs and a sloppy looking oversized T-shirt and handed them to Tyler.

Tyler took the cutoffs and with a big grin on his face, he said, "Let me try these on, but I'm not wearing any underwear today, so I'll have to make sure my dick don't hang out of the bottom of them. And thanks, but I'll go without a shirt – if a maternity shirt is all you have."

Zack looked at Tyler and grinned! "Yeah, yeah, don't hang out! Those damn cutoffs will almost hit your knees, how damn long do you think your dick is?"

Well with that comment, Tyler turned around and faced Zack with the shorts on only slightly above his ankles.

"Oh shit man!" Zack exclaimed. "Oh God Tyler I didn't realize that you were almost not kidding! Shit man, put that damn thing away unless you are going to sweep the floor with it. My God Tyler, how long is that damn thing?"

"Well, all I know is it's long enough to get me pretty well drunk when I was 19. That Robert I told you about, saw it in the rest room one day, and that is why he kind of set me up at his apartment that night. He knew about it, and he wanted to play with it. Of course I was real dumb and fell for it. I was set up, and I fell for the bait!"

"And you and that Robert never did it again after that? He never got to it again?"

"No. He was dropping out of training and some of his friends told him that unless he actually got me to his apartment, and got me to have sex with him, before he left, then they would not believe what he had been telling them, of what he had seen. So, well I guess he must have convinced them that we played together because whenever I saw any of his old buddies, I had to really tell them, 'No!' They all kept trying to get me to do stuff either with them, or for them."

"Uh, Tyler. How did he convince them that he actually got to you? Do you know?"

"No I really don't. And I think I know what you are thinking. I got too drunk and can't remember what happened. Right? You think maybe they were there later that night, and I just don't know it, right?"

"Right! Right you are! That was kind of before the "date rape drugs" but Tyler, I'll bet more guys have played with that dick than you know! I'll bet so!"

"I know Zack, I kind of think I agree! Too many guys made too many comments that I really don't think that Robert told them. I think he brought the others in after I got real drunk. Who did me, or what I did to them, I have no idea. That's one of the reasons why I refused to ever go with any of them."

Tyler finished pulling his cutoffs up, looked down and commented, "Well, as long as it don't get itself all excited, I guess it's kind of hidden."

Zack looked at Tyler and just shook his head.

As the two men headed out of the house and toward the stack of trash that Zack had already piled beside the shed, Tyler asked. "So Zack. Tell me about Kevin. What's he like, how long have you two been together and all that stuff!"

"Well, he's the same age as me, we're both 37. Knew him in high school back in Ohio, but never hung around him any until after we graduated. We really did not know each other, or should I say about each other, until one night about a year out of high school and we ran into each other in a gay bathhouse. Well, talk about a shock! Did not expect that, nor did he. So as you can imagine, whenever most people ask how we met, it's just simply, in "high school." No more details.

Zack's comment about the bath house really perked Tyler's attention.

"Zack, a gay bath house? Really? Zack, I want to know more. I've always heard about those places, but of course I've never been to one. What goes on there? Is there really open sex like I keep hearing? Is that true?"

Zack, looked at Tyler, grinned, grabbed his own crotch and said, "Oh man, let me tell you!"

As they gathered up the trash and loaded it into Tyler's truck, Zack related quite a number of stories about his experiences in different bath houses. Each story seemed to strike Tyler with a great amount of interest. Zack noticed. To Zack it did seem that each episode struck Tyler with more and more interest than the one before it! "These episodes really interest you, don't they?" Zack asked.

"Yeah, got to admit it Zack, they do, kind of. I've never had the opportunity to discuss this kind of stuff with any guy before, and that one night of my life has always made me want to find out more about that kind of stuff. Maybe I kind of learned just a little, but not enough to think I knew anything. So if you don't mind sharing with me, yeah, I kind of like learning some stuff. If there's anything that you don't want to tell me though, that's OK, I understand."

Zack continued to relate some of his bathhouse experiences and Tyler did ask a few questions. Tyler appreciated the sharing of experiences and stories that Zack was willing to share with him. He kept telling Zack that if it was something that he did not want to talk about, that was OK. Zack reassured him that by this time, he had pretty well heard just about all of the really far out stuff that he had done, so he really did not think there would be anything else that he, Zack, could not talk about. He told Tyler how excited he was about their new friendship and how they had so quickly gotten to know each other, and some pretty deep stuff about each of them. Tyler admitted that about the only deep thing that he had shared was his one night experience when he was nineteen, but yeah, he was enjoying the chance to get to know a lot of Zack's deep secrets.

The bed of the truck was finally full, and after throwing a plastic cover over it and tying it down, the two got in the cab and headed for a county dump that Zack said was not too far away.

\

Chapter Two:
Your Dick Must Think It Is Gay

As they drove, their conversations about Zack and Kevin's sexual experiences continued. Zack noticed that Tyler did not attempt to change the subject, and quite often asked something to rather keep the line of talk on the same subject.

During one rather interesting explanation of how Kevin and Zack had taken some young hot football player home and had a good long evening of gay sex with him, Zack noticed that just perhaps the cutoffs were not, in-fact, going to be long enough to hide the prized package that was hanging loosely inside. As Zack talked, he kept an eye on Tyler's crotch. Finally it happened! Tyler had gotten a hard-on and the tip was sticking out of the cutoffs. Tyler attempted to shift his leg so that it did not show, but to no avail.

"Tyler, for a straight guy, your dick must think it is gay, since it is responding to our conversation."

Tyler rose up a little in the seat so as to attempt to readjust everything. He did not say anything to Zack, but he did look over toward him and let out a slight grin.

"You're horny aren't you Tyler?" Zack asked.

Once again Tyler did not say anything. He once again grinned and then asked, as if he needed to, since the signs to the county dump were very evident, "Where do I turn?"

Zack grinned and replied, "You can turn anywhere you want, because I really don't think you can go as straight as you think you can!"

"Oh shit, nothing like putting my big foot right in my own mouth!" Tyler replied. "Zack, I have to admit, you are getting me all confused here man. Zack, as soon as you sat down across the table from me, I thought you were one hot looking guy, and I really did admire a lot about you. I, of course, did not know until we got to the house that you were a gay guy, but now that I do know, I'm feeling real confused. I'm married, I've got a beautiful wife, two great kids, and right now, I have to admit, I've got a real strong desire to jump in the sack with you. Zack, I'm confused. Yeah, there have been other times when I thought maybe I should try sex with another guy, but I always thought that was a result of that night with Robert – and whoever else was there, if there were other guys there, but today is different. Zack, I guess I should have never come over to Hillsburg today, or at least never invited you to join me at the table."

Tyler took a deep breath and looked over toward Zack. Zack was silent. He reached over and placed his hand on Tyler's upper leg. Tyler looked down at Zack's hand, then once again turned and looked at Zack. Zack saw a tear coming down the side of Tyler's cheek.

"Whoa Tyler. You OK man? Tyler pull over, pull off of the road man."

Tyler did, as he reached up and wiped the tear off of his cheek. He got the truck off of the side of the road and got it stopped. He dropped his head and again wiped another tear. "Oh God Zack, I'm so confused man! Zack I want to go to bed with you, but I'm not supposed to feel that way. Zack I'm married, I'm a daddy!" Suddenly Tyler broke out sobbing! Zack reached over and threw his arms around Tyler's shoulders. Tyler laid his head on Zack's shoulder, and as he truly sobbed, he said, "Zack, I've known for a long time that I wanted to have sex with a guy, and I've fought it for years. Zack I need help! I feel like I am going crazy man! Zack, can we go to your place and have sex. Zack, maybe if I do it once, then maybe I won't want to do it anymore. Oh Zack can you help me please?"

Zack hugged Tyler as tightly as he could; given the awkward position they were in, in the cab of the truck. Zack allowed Tyler to calmly sit there and cry as long as he needed to. Zack gave Tyler every bit of comfort that he could, and he calmly told Tyler that everything will be OK. He held Tyler until Tyler could regain his composure, and he then suggested that they move onto the county dump, get the truck unloaded and then go back to the house so they could sit and talk a little.

Tyler took a McDonald's napkin that had been lying on the seat and wiped his eyes. He took a deep breath, looked at Zack, slightly grinned, and kind of uttered, "OK."

Wiping his eyes again, Tyler looked at Zack and told him, "Oh shit man, I am sorry! Zack, my God man, I am so sorry!"

"No reason to be sorry Tyler, no reason at all!"

Tyler reached out to hug Zack, and Zack did likewise. For a couple of moments, or perhaps a couple of minutes, the two men sat there in the cab of the truck and hugged each other. As they broke their hug, Tyler kind of, very lowly said, "Well I guess that car load of people will have something to talk about now don't they?"

Zack replied, "Who gives a shit? Maybe they don't have any shit happening in their lives." He took hold of Tyler's chin, turned Tyler's face toward his own, and grinned.

Tyler rather shook his head as if to shake the cobwebs out of it put the truck in "Drive" and proceeded down the road.

Getting to the county dump, Tyler found a good spot where he could back the truck in to unload it, got it in place and turned the key off.

Zack reached over, put his hand in Tyler's crotch and asked, "Is everything tucked back in here OK before we get out of the truck?"

Tyler replied, "Oh hell yes! That damn thing went little and soft during my little episode back there."

"Just thought I'd make sure!" Zack said as they each got out of the truck. Within only a few minutes, they had the truck completely empty.

"Crap man! I wish it was as quick and as easy getting the crap in here as it is getting it out." Zack commented.

Tyler grinned, uttered a "Yeah," and after slamming the tail gate shut, they both got back in the cab.

As they left the county dump site, Tyler asked, "Well man, what else are you going to tell me about Kevin? I know he is your age, you guys met in school first, before you really met at the bath house, and he is an interior designer. What else?"

"Well," Zack responded. "Kevin is kind of a different kind of a guy! One look at him, and you could very easily ask which professional football team he plays for. He's a big strong man. He shoots down the normal concept of a gay interior designer. I often laugh and say – well if his clients don't want to do as he suggests, then he can just squeeze them until they agree with him. It looks like you and I are about the same size, I mean you can wear my cutoffs, but Kevin; well he's about probably another ninety or a hundred pounds – and all muscles! He weighs in, right at about, two seventy-five. Six foot two, black flat top haircut, and a square jaw just like Dick Tracy used to have. Tyler – to me he is one hell of a hot man! He takes a lot of shit about his profession, but they shut up pretty fast if he gets a frown on his face.

As they drove home, Zack attempted to keep the subject on the light and fluffy side, so as to not get Tyler upset again.

Zack told Tyler that one load to the dump was enough for that day. He suggested that they go in and get something good and refreshing to drink and take a quick shower and get out of the dusty and dirty clothes that they had on.

"OK." Tyler said as Zack made his suggestions as to what they were going to do. "I'll shower, but you've going to shower with me, OK?"

"Tyler, are you real sure that is something that we should do?" Zack asked.

"Yes Zack, I am sure. I am damn sure! I have put off something like this happening for me for way too damn long now, and today, and with you, is the closest thing I've had happen that gives me a chance. Zack, I want to do it to see what my reactions are. I need to know!"

"OK if you insist, but Tyler, don't do anything that you know you should not be doing."

"Zack, I need to be doing this! You saw the way I acted in the truck. I've been fighting this for years now, and maybe it's time for me to confront the who I really am! Maybe it will be a real turn off to me, but then maybe not. I need to find out once and for all!"

As Zack told him OK, they then proceeded upstairs and shed their dirty clothes. Zack went into the bathroom and turned on the shower and waited long enough to adjust the water temperature.

Tyler came into the shower, and he looked at Zack from top to bottom. He then said, "Well shit man! You were making comments about the length of my dick, and you sure are hanging a long one yourself." And with that comment, Tyler reached out and took Zack's dick in his hand. He squeezed it and then started stroking it back and forth. Zack did not say anything, he just stood there, letting the water hit his back, and letting Tyler handle his dick. As he did stand there, and with Tyler stroking his cock, it did start to get hard. He watched and noticed that although Tyler's cock was already starting to get firm as he entered the shower stall, it was now standing at an almost total vertical stand. Zack reached out and took it in his hand. He squeezed it and watched Tyler's face.

Tyler smiled at the feeling of having Zack grabbing his rod. Tyler moaned a low, "Oh yeah, oh yeah!" Zack watched as Tyler let his head fall back, as he enjoyed the feeling of Zack having a hold of his dick, and he in return having Zack's cock stick in his hand. With his head tipped fully back, and his eyes closed, Tyler again said, "Oh yes man. Oh yes!"

Zack reached up with his other hand and placed a finger and a thumb on Tyler's left tit. Watching Tyler's face, he slightly squeezed. Tyler smiled broadly, and openly spoke saying, "Oh God yes man! Oh God that feels so good! Oh God Zack, pinch it, pinch it man!"

Zack now had Tyler's ragging hard-on in one hand and a tit in the other hand, and Tyler's hand firmly grasping his hard and stiff rod. The shower water was hitting Zack's back, and also hitting Tyler's face and chest. Tyler still had his face tipped back, and Zack could tell that Zack was in complete joy with – where he was at, and with – what he was doing. Although he already knew the answer, Zack asked. "You OK man? You OK?"

"Oh God yes I am! Oh shit Zack, yes I am! Oh Zack pinch my tit! Yeah man, yeah play with it. Oh Zack this is great, Oh Zack I've wanted this for a long time, yeah man, pinch me and jerk my dick!"

Zack did as he had been requested to do. It sent Tyler into some very high highs. He kept moaning and groaning about how great it felt, and kept asking for more, and more. Zack lowered his hand from Tyler's tit, and putting it around his waist he pulled him forward and gave him a very large hug. While hugging Tyler tightly, Zack lowered his face and gave Tyler a very firm kiss on the neck. Tyler leaned in to accept the kiss and at the same time squeezed Zack's cock even that much harder.

Zack let loose of Tyler's cock and his waist and reached around him and firmly placed a hand on each hip. He grabbed each butt muscle very firmly so that he would know Tyler had to definitely feel it, and he squeezed. Slowly he kept moving each hand in so slowly toward the middle line of Tyler's ass. As his hands moved inward, they also continued to slightly spread Tyler's ass cheeks. Slowly Zack's hands each reached the spot that Zack had been heading for, and that was the small opening, so neatly hidden between the two large muscles. Slowly Zack moved each hand inward and allowed his fingers to find the choice spot. First one finger slid in, and then immediately the second finger followed suit. Tyler sunk onto Zack's chest. He moaned a very pronounced, "Oh my God yeah!"

Tyler was in the process of, for his very first time in his life, getting the fingers of another man slid up, and into, his asshole. For so many years he had wondered just what this would feel like, and now he was finding out. He was finding out it was an indescribable heaven. He was melting as he felt Zack gently search around inside of his ass. Tyler had never dreamt that having some man put his finger up in his ass end, could possibly feel so outrageously good!

As Tyler was getting his ass filled with a couple of fingers, he had let loose of Zack's cock, and had placed his hands up under Zack's arm pits and was hugging him by having a firm hold on Zack's upper back. This allowed Tyler to completely feel Zack, body to body, almost from the feet up all of the way to the neck, but it also brought his bare and warmly wet body even that much closer to Zack, so that Zack could insert into his asshole any number of fingers that Zack wanted to share.

Zack softly said, "Do me!" Tyler knew immediately what Zack meant. He lowered his hands from up along Zack's shoulder blades, and allowed them to gently slide down Zack's back, across the top of his hips, reach in toward the center line of Zack's ass and so very slowly and very carefully start the loving journey in-between the two massive muscles that make up Zack's hot ass. Tyler placed the tips of his fingers in-between the butt muscles. Slowly, he extended his finger out to reach for the warm inner spaces of the anatomy section called – Zack's butt. As he approached the golden zone getting closer and closer to Zack's asshole, he could feel Zack hug him tighter and tighter and push more finger length up into his own ass. He knew that Zack now had the tip of four fingers roaming around at his ass opening. He could feel two fingers on each side roaming and pulling, attempting to get the little hole comfortably open just a little more on each tug. The feeling was way beyond anything else that Tyler had ever experienced before. He wondered if on that night, back when he was 19, and drunk out of his mind, had anything like this happened to him back then. If so, and he had no conscious memory of it, was his unconscious memory the item that had been directing him toward this action and discovery. Tyler was not unhappy that he had told Zack that he wanted to try some gay sex. Tyler felt this was completely natural and normal. He was only so very disappointed in himself that he had not allowed this to happen many, many, years ago. As he continued to enjoy the outrageous joys of not only feeling Zack's ass, and allowing his fingers to approach ever so carefully his asshole, he was in complete joy over the feelings he was having encouraging Zack's fingers to do the roaming and prying in his asshole. As he enjoyed this piece of heaven, he mentally ran a history of the many times in the past that he could have maybe worked out something like this, with other guys, if he had just allowed it to happen.

Chapter Three:
Out of His Head With Excitement

Tyler remembered the day with the appliance workman that really tried to come on to him when they were working alone in a recently completed house. Tyler remembered hot, nice looking, and how well built that man was, and how he had questioned himself for the next couple of days about why in the hell didn't he let that man go for it. He decided that when one man pretty well comes straight out and tells you how you "look like fun," he's pretty hot for some action. Tyler had decided later that he had really screwed up on that one!

Then there was the trim, firm, swimmer's body lifeguard in the dressing room at the city pool. Oh how Tyler had always regretted his rather stupid move of brushing that hunk off. Tyler could still, to this day, some 8 or 9 years later, remember how that lifeguard had simply stood there, squarely in front of him, and openly rubbed his own crotch as an out and out signal and offer that – I'm open for sex! Tyler relived that day for years and years, and actually decided that he must still be reliving it, since he could remember it so clearly today. Tyler remembered how terribly disappointed that lifeguard looked when he shook his head "No," and said, "I'm straight!" Tyler could only explain his reason for rejecting the offer was that he was 24 or maybe 25 at the time, and he simply knew the lifeguard could not have been more than 18, and at that time in your life, that is a big age difference. "Oh, to have had that chance again, more recently!" He thought to himself.

"So many stupid times when I could have done this, with so many other guys! And they were all hot looking guys! God, how dumb am I?" Tyler questioned himself as he rather came back around to the reality of what was then happening. He had four fingers up in his ass, he was hugging one hell of a hot looking and hot built man, and besides, he was reaching for that man's asshole! He was in the process of all of this – and he was thinking about the times that he did not do it. "Forget the past stupid – get with the now," he scolded himself.

As Zack was pulling him closer and closer to get more and more finger length, and fingers, up in Tyler's ass, he was almost pulling Tyler up off of the floor. Tyler was continuing to progressively move more and more butt muscle out of the way so that he could see what it felt like to put his fingers up in another man's ass. He hugged Zack firmly in every attempt to reach that magic spot.

Bango! He was there! Tyler felt the edge of Zack's asshole. He let one finger from his right hand poke in. "Oh man that feels like I'm sticking it in the side of a warm juicy melon! Oh man, I like that!" He emotionally said to the receiver of his finger. Slowly he pushed his other hand toward the direction of the warm hole. That finger found its target and Tyler pushed it in beside the first finger.

"Oh man. Oh God!" Tyler almost kind of screamed. "Oh God this feels as good as getting fingers up in your own ass! Oh Zack! I've got my fingers up in your asshole! Oh Zack, can I pull on your ass? Oh man can I try to pull your asshole open?"

"Oh yeah man! Yeah, play with my butt hole. Put those fingers up in me, let me feel you tug on my butt hole. Yeah Tyler, play with my butt!"

The two men were in complete glory feeling each other and getting up inside of each other's asses. Zack was much more used to this action than Tyler was, of course, but knowing that he was giving something to Tyler, that he had never had before, definitely enlarged the excitement for Zack.

Tyler was already almost out of his head with excitement. He had dreamed of maybe feeling this with a guy for so long now that he was having some real trouble realizing that it was actually happening. He was finally arm in arm, hand in hand, or maybe we should say – hand in ass, with another hot hunky and bare assed man, and he was being given the opportunity to feel and play with that man in any and every way that he could. He was living something that he could never have imagined possible.

As Zack continued to finger Tyler's asshole, he lowered his head down and took Tyler's right nipple into his mouth. He sucked on it as if he was feeding off of his Mommy. Tyler once again almost wilted. He was glad that Zack had a firm grip on his ass. He needed the strength and support to remain standing. This new and expounded feeling on his chest made Tyler push his fingers up and into Zack's butt hole that much more forcefully. He could feel the inside of Zack's ass and it was turning him on completely.

Zack chewed and sucked on Tyler's right nipple and then did the same to his left nipple. Tyler kept moaning more and more pleasures as Zack took care of his body. Tyler laid his head on Zack's shoulder and started licking his neck as if he was a dog licking his master. Zack encouraged Tyler to finger his ass and to lick his neck to his complete enjoyment!

Slowly Zack moved his face down the front of Tyler's body, licking as he went. Keeping his fingers in Tyler's ass, Zack continued to lower himself down, and started licking Tyler's stomach area and then his crotch area. With the side of his face, he pushed Tyler's hard-on to the side so that he could lick on the skin right beside it. Tyler of course had to pull his hands back, and allow his fingers to come back out of Zack's ass, but he used them to caress and rub Zack's shoulders and his neck to let the hunky man know that everything that was happening was feeling great, really great!

Zack continued to lower himself down even farther and after letting his fingers slip out of Tyler's warm asshole, he grabbed the back of his legs, and he positioned himself so that he could start licking the insides of Tyler's legs, starting right beneath Tyler's bag. He let his head move the soft flexible bag out of the way and he strongly pushed his tongue up against Tyler's inside upper thigh, up right beside his bag and started licking. This feeling of Zack's tongue right at the top of his leg, and right beside his bag made Tyler shiver. Tyler once again went limp. He grabbed for the shower head to support himself! He moaned in pleasure and he again told Zack of how wonderfully great he felt with Zack taking him as his own. "Zack lick me! Zack chew on me! Zack you are making me feel so good! Oh Zack, I can't believe this!"

Tyler stood there with the warm shower water hitting him directly in the face and then running off of him to land on Zack, squatting down below. Tyler liked this happening since he kind of felt like it was an offering from him, to Zack. A small offering, but none the less, something that had at first been on him, and was now going on to Zack, and Zack was maybe getting some of that water into his mouth. Tyler felt that in some funny way, he was sharing a part of himself with Zack. He watched the water drip from his body onto Zack's shinny body, as he enjoyed the feel of the hunky man licking his legs and the feelings of having that man's head touching his bare skin and his bag of nuts.

Zack enjoyed feeling Tyler's leg skin, down one leg and then back up and then down the second. He then stood up and Tyler knew it was now his turn to be the licking person, and it was his turn to feel some manly meat on his tongue. Without saying anything at all, he started his slow and deliberate trip down Zack's chest, onto his stomach, around his dick area, and as he took a very deep breath, he placed his face up against Zack's dick and his bag. He had never been in this position before. He was squatting there now, with the water dripping off of Zack and onto him, and he was about to touch a man's dick and this man's balls with his face. Silently but mentally Tyler said to himself, "Oh my God, I am going to put my mouth on this man's cock! Oh God, I never thought I'd ever get to do this!"

Zack had his hands on top of Tyler's head. He was encouraging Tyler, ever so gently, by rubbing on the top of his head. Zack knew what Tyler was going through. He knew what Tyler had on his mind at that time. He remembered back many years earlier when he, for the very first time, let his mouth touch another guy's crotch. He remembered how young he was at that time, and the crotch that he put his face on – was the most exciting part of the young assistant coach at college. It was after a baseball practice, and Zack had helped the field crew on the diamond after the practice. The twenty-four year old coach did not know that Zack had not yet come in and showered down. At that time, everybody else had showered down, dressed and left.

Zack remembered that on that day, when he came into the locker room, the assistant coach was taking a warm soapy shower, and with the shower water running, he did not hear Zack come in. Much to his shock and total embarrassment, Zack walked in just as the coach was jerking himself off. Zack stood there and gasped as the coach got all flustered and tried to say it was not what it really looked like. Zack had been way too much 'taken' to just let it pass. He went into the shower, even with his baseball pants still on, and stood by the coach and stared at him. He had never seen this assistant coach completely bare, nor of course, had he ever seen his cock, even soft, let alone hard. Hard, as it was then, it was a very strong and thick eight inch dick. The coach was in shock of what was happening and he simply stood there, with his dick in hand! He had not intended for any of his students to see anything like this. Zack was so excited about what he was looking at, he reached out, took a hold of the coach's dick and knelt down in front of it. The coach tried to tell him "No, No," but Zack remembered he would not listen. Zack remembered how he had told the coach, "Yes, I have to do this, or I will tell!"

Having Tyler on his knees in front of his crotch and knowing that this was Tyler's first time brought back a lot of very fine memories. Zack truly enjoyed remembering the way he managed to suck on that assistant coach, his first man! Now he knew it was Tyler's turn, although, as a much older man than he personally had been. He could only hope that in the future, Tyler would have as many opportunities to re-suck his first man, has he personally had. "Good thought!" Zack thought to himself. "Especially since I am his first man! That means he returns often, and sucks on me! Now that would be great!"

Tyler had been moving his way around the exciting parts of Zack's body as Zack slipped back into history and fondly remembered his first blow job on the coach. Tyler was slowly working his way back up Zack's right leg, very carefully licking and enjoying every square inch of it. He slowly continued his move up the leg, and Zack could see him looking upward as if to wonder how close I am to his cock and balls. Zack reached down and slapped Tyler on the head with his hard-on. That made Tyler look up. Zack did it again. Tyler grinned. Zack then took hold of his rod, and pushing it down, he aimed it toward Tyler's face. Tyler's eyes got kind of wide, and he took a very, very deep breath.

Zack simply asked, "Ready?" He pushed it down farther to more correctly aim it directly toward Tyler's mouth. Slowly and very carefully Tyler rose up some from on his knees, and moved his mouth toward the dick. He continued to hold onto Zack's legs. Zack aimed the dick, and Tyler positioned his mouth to accept it. Slowly Tyler moved forward and let the tip of it go into his mouth. Slowly Zack moved forward and let slightly more of it slide in. "Good, yeah!" Exclaimed Zack! "Yeah, good man! Lick the tip!"

As Tyler knelt there, he kept ahold of Zack's legs, and he very nervously ran his tongue around the outside of Zack's dick. Zack slightly moved his body forward to assist Tyler in taking more and more of his dick, but without freaking Tyler out by feeding him too much cock, too fast.

The shower water continued to hit Zack on his upper back, and on his shoulders and then fall on down to hit Tyler. Tyler knew he was now in the process of sucking on Zack's rod, but for some funny reason the falling water, coming off of Zack's body, and then, on down, to fall on him, was almost as sexual as sucking on the meat stick.

Slowly but very deliberately, Zack managed to get almost his entire dick into Tyler's mouth before Tyler choked and had to pull off of it to cough. "I think you got some water in your mouth Tyler. I think that is what made you choke." Zack told Tyler.

"I don't think so!" Tyler finally responded once he got done choking. "I had that damn big dick of yours in my mouth! That is what I was choking on! It wasn't any water, it was that damn big telephone pole that I was trying to eat." With a grin on his face and a grin in his voice, he then told Zack. "When you are swinging that much dick in some guy's mouth, don't blame it on water!"

As Tyler was expounding on the size of the dick that he had been sucking on, Zack had reached down and by putting his hands under Tyler's arm pits, he had lifted him up.

"You did good man!" Zack said. "Tyler, I have to admit it kind of shocked me that you even attempted to take my dick the very first time you played around. Usually it will take a guy a few play sessions before he finally decides to put some guy's dick in his mouth, but you really were ready to see what's up, weren't you? You not only took it the first chance you got, but you sure took a lot of it. Tyler, I've fucked a lot of mouths before that sure can't take as much of that dick as you did. And those are guys that supposedly have sucked cock for years. You did good! How you feeling?"

As Tyler stood there, he hugged Zack and listened to what Zack had to say. "I'm OK. Yeah, really, I'm OK. Zack, this was a lot more exiting and heart pounding than I thought it would be. I'm really pissed at myself that I never did this before, but I sure am glad I finally did it. This is good! No, I guess I should say, this is great! This is really great! This is hot! This kind of sex is a hell of a lot more exciting than the straight stuff, don't you think?"

"Tyler, I can't honestly answer that. I've never had sex with a woman. I've never had any interest in doing that, so I can't say. I will tell you though that you are not the first guy that usually does women that I have played with, and you sure are not the first one to say the same thing. I guess men just know how to satisfy another man. Besides us just standing here, getting wet, what do you want to do? You want to play some more, or are you ready to call it quits. You name it man, it's your call."

Tyler looked at Zack and asked. "It's my call? It's really my call?"

Zack answered, "Yeah."

"OK then, I want to get sucked off. I want you to do me, and make me cum. I want you to finger my ass some more, and let me do yours if it's OK with you. Can we maybe go to the bed though, and get out of the water. Is it OK if you and I go to bed together. I mean, if you and Kevin have some kind of an agreement that you don't do that kind of stuff when the other person is not here, I understand, but if we can, I sure would love it!"

"OK, but you've got to let me fuck you, OK? I've got this funny little saying I try to stick to, and it goes – 'In my bed, and in your butt!' "

"What! You wanna fuck me? Is that what you said?"

"Yeah, yeah. Yeah you've got me all hot and bothered here, and now I need myself some ass. Willing? You willing?"

"Oh shit man. Oh Zack, you know I've never had anything up in my butt hole before. I'm not sure I can do that!"

"Hey man, really there ain't no man nowhere that can't get it up in the butt if he's just willing. Seriously man, all you gotta do is decide you want it, and believe me, once you get it, you're gonna be yelling for more! I'm not kidding, you will love it! I'll suck you off, and then you just lay there and let me do my thing back there? OK?"

"Oh shit Zack! You really sure I can take that dick of yours up in my ass? You sure?"

"Tyler, I've never gone for one yet that I've not been able to put my ole dick up in. Come here man, give me that dick. I got some serious sucking to do here. OK?"

"Yeah, I guess, I guess. This is really turning me on man, I gotta get sucked off, so I guess I'm willing. But please! When you start fucking me, if I really can't take it, promise to quit, please?!"

"No problem with that problem, cause I got total faith that once the tip of my dick starts touching the edge of your asshole, you're gonna realize that you've been worrying about something for no reason at all. Face it man, you know you want to do it. Remember our conversation in the truck? See, you're wanting it, you just keep thinking that you need to keep finding reasons to not do it! You're gonna be OK, believe me. I wouldn't tell you so if it wasn't true! Here man, lie down here. Lie down and relax."

Tyler laid down on the bed and let Zack get at, and get ahold of his rod. The ole pole was standing straight up in the air, and Zack was finally getting the hunk of meat in his mouth that he'd been looking at, and he was now 'taking care of it.'

For ten or maybe fifteen minutes, Zack gave Tyler the experience of a lifetime getting his rod sucked on as strongly as any man has ever had.

"Oh man, oh man!" Tyler finally let out, just at about the time that he grabbed a stronger hold on Zack's head and tried to ram his cock back into the back of his mouth as far as he could ram it, and then let out a very long drawn-out, "Oh shit man, oh shit – I'm gonna cum man – I'm gonna cum! Oh man, oh man! Oh shit Zack, I came! Oh man did I cum! Oh wow man that felt so fucking damn good!"

After Tyler managed to re-coop some from his extensive cumming climax, and after Zack got a chance to regain some breath and strength after sucking on Tyler like he was trying to suck all of the air out of a hot air balloon, Zack told him to flop – gut down – on the bed, and get ready for his first, 'cock-up-in-the-ass' session. Still expressing some pretty strong concerns about if he really could take a dick up in the ass or not, he did lie down and Zack took his top man position, right above his ass.

"Just lie there and relax. I'm gonna grease that cute little ass of yours, and my dick, up with some good slippery grease, and then I'm just gonna go real slow and let you finally find out just how great having some guy's dick stuck up in your ass can feel."

Slowly, Zack did progress. That was until he had the whole length of his rod up and in Tyler's ass and all of a sudden, he knew he should have been born with a much longer dick because, what he had, was just not turning out to be enough to satisfy Tyler's begging for fucking him harder, deeper and stronger!

"Oh my God man, oh my God! Oh Zack fuck me man, fuck me! Oh shit how in the hell could I have ever been afraid to do this!? Oh yeah man, oh yeah! Do me – do me, yeah do me hard! Fuck me man fuck me! Fuck me hard! Stick it in me man – stick it in me!"

With that begging for more – more, harder – harder, and deeper – deeper, Zack had no doubt that he was now taking care of one man and one ass that had been wanting this for a hell of a long time, but just had never had the right time nor the right man standing by.

On his gut, on his hands and knees, and then even on his back with his legs up in the air and wrapped around Zack's shoulders, Tyler started making up for some lost time, and some lost opportunities. He was getting fucked in every possible position and way that he could get it, and he was still begging for more.

With Tyler's legs up and on his shoulders, Zack told him, "Hang on man, I'm about to let you have it up in the ole butt with some more of my cum stuff! I'm gonna do it, I'm gonna do it! Oh shit man, oh shit! Oh Tyler, your ass has just been bred! I just unloaded in there man, I did! If you were some kind of a female that could get bred in the ass, you'd be carrying probably about ten of my kids up in there right now! Oh shit man, I unloaded in you – I did. Your ass was way too hungry for that man, it was! I don't know how many years you've been waiting for something like that, but man, you got it today! You OK? Your ass okay?"

It took both men about ten minutes of just lying there and re-cooping some before either man could make any serious effort of attempting to move some.

Finally Tyler reached over, grabbed onto Zack's rod, jerked it back and forth a few times and said, "Zack, I'm gonna be needing this thing back up in me again, and again and again. I cannot tell you how fucking hot and exciting that was for me. I'm sorry I did all of that whining about how I didn't think I could take that! I guess I just been saying that to myself for so many years now, that I actually believed it! Thank you, thank you!"

"Hey, thank you back man, thank you! You got one hell of a hot ass, and I'm gonna want it again, and again, and again too! How we gonna work that out? How we gonna do that?"

Today I used the back roads so I could take a nice calm drive, but it'll only take me about fifteen minutes if I use the highway, and believe me man, I will now be using the highway over this direction probably more than once a week, if you'll have me. Will you? Can I come over just as often as I can, and get the same good deep and rough treatment like I did today?"

"Hell yes man, hell yes! Thank goodness today was your day playing like being a bachelor, cause man, this day has changed a lot for you, and is making my life one hell of a lot more active and exciting. I've been looking for a hot ass like yours for a long time now, and now – I finally found it! Thanks Tyler, thanks for being here and believing me when I told you that once it went in up in there, that you were gonna be begging for more."

"Zack my man, I did, and I still am! I want it again before I leave today, and then at least twice a week after that – and I mean, each week! Thanks Zack, thanks! God alive man – thank goodness you had some trash that needed to be hauled away. I'll love hauling trash for the rest of my life!"

THE VEGAS THING

Chapter One:
The Hotel is Still Officially Closed

"Hey Chad, Tim, thanks for coming in men. Hey, guys, here's the deal. I got a call from one of the guys in the Owners/Managers group that I belong to. He told me that there is a hotel in Vegas that is being remodeled and they're not getting it all done in time for the Electronics Convention. It's an eight story hotel with about 300 rooms in it. The owners of the hotel have made a deal with our mangers group to rent out the rooms under a very particular, and peculiar arrangement."

As Chad and Tim sat there, they were hearing some very interesting information, from Mr. Stoneburn, the store owner, about hotel rooms for the upcoming Electronics convention in Las Vegas.

Mr. Stoneburn continued, "First, very cheap rates for the convention! They would just like to get the room staff back to working as soon as possible, and they figure that if they make this special deal, then they will be able to put them back to work and pay them. Now the people that do stay there will have to sign an agreement, stating that they understand the hotel is not fully functional. There's no cafeteria, nor food service, there's no athletic club, nor health facilities, they may have to step around workers and tools, there's no phone system up and running yet, but they figure since most everybody uses cell phones today, that shouldn't be a problem. They cannot guarantee how many people will be in a room. It's going to be kind of like summer camp. You take what you get. It may be a room with two twins beds, it might be a room with one double bed, or it might be a room with two double beds. If you guys decide that you want to go to the convention and use this place, we don't know what your rooming arrangements will be for sure. We won't know until you get there. You might have a room to yourselves, and then you might have two other guys in the same room. The bathrooms are fully functional, the towels and sheets and all that type of stuff is there and will be provided, but no room service, nor mini bars in the rooms yet, no wakeup call service, and although there definitely will be beds and dressers, some rooms may yet be lacking some side furniture such as side chairs. Some of the public spaces, like the hallways, will not be painted or finished yet. The hotel is not open for reservations. If a person tries to make a room reservation, the hotel is still officially closed. One of the owners knows one of the electronics convention guys, and he's doing this in an attempt to help get some of his people back to work sooner, and he's also doing this to give some people, that might not be able to attend the convention, a real cheap room rate so they can attend."

"Both of you guy are young and I figure you two can kind of go with the flow – so to say – if you are interested. I don't think I would have suggested this to some older guys that expect everything to be given to them on a silver platter. Now, if you guys are interested in this deal, I'll pay for the room and the flight tickets, but everything else, food and all the other expenses are on your own. Are you interested?"

Chad looked over at Tim, then back at Mr. Stoneburn and immediately said, "Yes! Yes I'm interested!"

Then looking at Tim, Chad continued with, "Tim, you game man? You interested?"

Mr. Stoneburn interrupted. "Hey wait a minute guys! Wait a minute! I forgot one rather important point that I should have pointed out! I can only do this if both of you guys are interested. See, I have to sign up and pay for two guys minimum, since each room takes at least two guys. If one of you is not interested, then I have to apologize and pull the offer back. I'm sorry, I have to pay for at least two people or more."

"Hey not a problem men!" Tim quickly replied. "I'm sorry I didn't answer a little quicker. Yeah – yes, I'm definitely interested. I've wanted to go to the electronic convention for years now, but I've never been able to afford the room rates, so yes – I'm definitely interested! Sounds like a hell of a good deal to me!"

"Great men! I'll call Sam, the guy that called me about this and tell him I've got two guys set to go. He'll need to fax me the statements that you guys need to sign, to state that you both understand the particular situation associated here. As soon as I get them, I'll have you guys come back in and sign them so we can get them turned back in. Okay?"

"Yeah definitely!" Chad and Tim both expressed as they each got up and thanked Mr. Stoneburn again for doing this for them.

As they left Mr. Stoneburn's office, Chad excitedly looked at Tim and said, "Man this is great! Tim, I have always wanted to go to the convention but man, I can't afford those room rates that week! Man this is great! Are you as excited about this as I am?"

"Yeah I guess I am, Chad, but you've got to remember, for you it's just you, and for me – well this is going to be kind of a surprise to Jenny when I go home and tell her I'm going to the convention for four or five days, and we never even talked about the possibility of me doing that."

"Oh Tim, you don't think she'll be upset do you? She'll be glad you can do this – right?"

"Yeah, I'm sure it will be okay. Just kind of a surprise though. Well hell man, right now it's a surprise to me too."

"Uh Tim, Mr. Stoneburn, he did tell us that we MIGHT be in a room that only has one double bed, or maybe a room that has two double beds, but then two other guys too, Right? If we do end up in a situation where you and I have to sleep in the same bed, is that okay with you? Is that a problem?"

As Tim jokingly stepped back, took a full length look up and down Chad, he then laughingly replied, "I don't think so man, I really don't think that will be tooooo much of a problem!"

"Well shit man, I'm not that fucking ugly am I?" Chad laughed, in response.

"No you ain't that fucking ugly, but unless you are one hell of a good cross-dresser, you sure don't have the equipment that would create a problem for me, being in bed with it!"

Chad and Tim were co-workers, salesmen really, in an upper-scale "novelty shop" that catered to men that needed to own the latest of whatever was on the market for the men that had way too many big boy toys! The store did not have cars, but just about any other type of "prestige – I've got it and you don't," – type of electronic or office type of item.

Chad, of course, was still a single guy. Aged 26, former "all-round" school athlete since the school was small enough to where the "good" athletes played all of the sports – whichever sport was in season, so to say. His body definitely did ring athlete! And his face rang handsome, definitely handsome! Some of the "store talk" had always been, behind the cupboards talk that is, that Chad was still single since he was so damn well built and so damn handsome, that he intimidated the gals. Then, of course, some others just felt that since he seemed to have so much going for him, that he was just plain happy "playing the field."

Tim was 29, married to Jenny, and had one son by the name of Timmy Jr. Tim's appearance was much more to the normal side of the scale. Five foot eleven, about 175 or 180 pounds and looked much more like he could have been more of a swimmer in his younger years. Nice looking guy, just nothing that somebody from across the room would make a fuss over.

Chad and Tim were the more experienced salesmen in the store. The other five sales individuals were all hired within the last year and a half, and since Chad and Tim had been there since the day Mr. Stoneburn opened the store, four years earlier, it was not out of reason that they got the trip to the convention.

The three weeks of looking forward to the convention trip went by quite quickly and with much anticipation. Jenny had no problem with Tim going, and she actually acted much more excited about it than he did, since she simply knew that his going was going to make him that much more successful in the store. Since Mr. Stoneburn, Chad and Tim were all going to be gone for four or five days, the store limited its normal open hours with the explanation that the three would be attending the electronics convention. This definitely was to the approval of their store customers, since the store customers definitely felt that with the three men being in attendance, they would be made immediately aware of any and all new "electronic toys" that had just hit the market.

Checking into the "hotel" was a rather unusual and different experience. Mr. Stoneburn's explanation of this being like summer camp was pretty much on the mark. There was no front check-in counter. As they approached the front door, a man standing there asked them if they had "papers." Understanding that he meant the page they had been issued after their signed statement of understanding this was not a fully functioning hotel, he then checked a list, and told them they would use room 410.

"Oh guys! They are working okay today, but while you are here, the elevators may not always be working. If you hit the button, and the light does not come on, it's stairs time, okay?"

Tim looked at Chad, Chad returned the glance, both smiled and Tim replied. "Okay, yeah okay!"

Then looking at Chad, he added, "My god! Thank goodness, room 410, not 810!"

Chad replied, "Yeah – right!"

"Yeah – right – but——?"

"But what?" Chad asked as Tim did not finish his statement.

With a very big grin on his face, Tim looked at Chad and in a very jokingly manner replied, "Yeah but – I saw you in those Speedos last summer at the company swim party, and eight flights of stairs wouldn't hurt that tight ass of yours at all anymore. Chad, you aren't running the stairs like you used to, are you?"

"Shit man! Shit! You trying to tell me my butt is getting fat or something? Is that what you are telling me?"

"No not fat, not fat! Just not as hard rock solid as it was when we first met. That's all I'm saying!"

"Tim what in the hell are you saying man? What are you saying? Why in the hell would you know what my ass looked like when we first met?"

"Chad – face it man! When you came to town, I'm fucking surprised your face wasn't pictured on the front page of the newspaper. You were, well still are, the hottest thing walking around, and I and everybody else checked you out as much as we could. Yes man, hell yes, I checked you out at that first swim party we were at together. Me and every other fucking person there did. Chad, then, your ass looked like two boulders stuck under those trunks. All I'm saying is – Chad my man, your ass is more like a normal person's ass now. That's all, I'm just glad you are finally becoming one of us, one of the normal people!"

"Shit man, shit! Tim, are you fucking with me man? You fucking with my head or something man? I'm no different than anybody else. I'm just me!"

"I know, I know! Let's face it Chad. You have got the body of death on you, and I have been jealous of it ever since we met. So of course I'm anxious for you to lose some of your "athletic body." Chad, I didn't mean anything by what I said. I just noticed that your ass is not as tight and as solid on you as it used to be, and hey – hell yeah – I'm glad. That's all I was commenting about! Hey – here's 410. Well – ready to see what our room is like?"

As they opened the door, Chad looked around and said, "Well, does this mean we will have roommates?"

"I guess I have to assume so, don't you think? Two double beds! I guess. From everything I've heard, this place did fill up with employees from the group Joe, I mean – Mr. Stoneburn belongs to, so I assume there will be two more in here. Right now I'm glad you suggested that we make sure we each have a suitcase that locks so we can lock up anything we need to and not let anything laying out. We have no idea who may be staying here at all."

"Yeah, I know Tim, but I don't think I'm too concerned since we do know it has to be somebody from that Managers organization. It's got to be one of their people, not just somebody that made a reservation."

"Yeah right! Yeah – you're right. And besides the room is really in a whole hell of a lot better shape than I thought it might be. Looks to me like this room is completely ready for opening day. I don't see anything missing from in here, do you?"

"Just the stuff that is normally in the mini bar. It's still empty."

"Hey Chad, look! Here's a note that's kind of interesting! Call this number and you can have somebody deliver a six pack of domestic beer and a bag of potato chip, or popcorn, for $15, paid at the door when he delivers it. Can't be charged to a card, but if you want a six pack and chips or popcorn, for $15 bucks, they will deliver. Hey – not too bad. Makes the beer like two bucks each, but hey, what would we pay if we went to a bar? Probably more than that!"

After "getting slightly settled" into the hotel room, Chad and Tim hit the road to find some grub for supper. Upon their return they did discover that true to their anticipation, they would be sharing the room with two others – Ben and Greg.

Ben and Greg, as they discovered during their get aquatinted conversation, were co-workers from a company in San Diego. Greg was the department supervisor, and Ben was one of those that reported to Greg. They were part of the sales staff. The four roommates all got along very well, they had a lot in common to talk about since they were all in the electronics business, although Tim and Chad did stick together pretty tightly as did Ben and Greg, which would of course be rather expected.

The pairing of all four did seem to be a good fit, since all four men did seem to have a little more than just the electronics in common, including ages – well, almost. Ben, anyway was in their age bracket, he was 25, but Greg was slightly older, being just shy of turning 40.

Ben was definitely the jock type as was Chad, and Greg was much more the business type of person, although a rather well built business man – from what could be seen through the normal casual business attire that he normally wore. Ben, obviously preferred to look much more casual and informal in sportier clothes. His pull over T-shirts covered a very, very fine body and chest structure. It was kind of obvious that he enjoyed letting others see and admire his structure. Tim and Chad had noticed that if Ben did wear a sports jacket, his only shirt was a very skin tight T-shirt type of shirt, but maybe one with a little more class than just a regular cotton shirt.

All four men did some tours of the convention booths together a few times, and shared some common time when lunch or dinner time approached.

The four sharing the same room did seem to be rather a good combination.

Chapter Two:
No Great Surprises Happened Until –

No great surprises happened until – until late Tuesday afternoon, when Chad and Tim did return to the room quite a little earlier than expected.

Much to everybody's surprise, as Chad and Tim entered the room, they discovered that Ben and Greg were definitely much closer friends than just being co-workers. And definitely much, much closer than just supervisor and subordinate.

"Oh shit guys, oh God man, we're sorry! Oh God man! We didn't think you guys were planning on coming back until after supper! God man, we're sorry!" Ben exclaimed with vigor and emphasis. "Oh man we didn't think you guys were coming back so soon! I thought you were going to be out till later today!"

Chad and Tim walked in just as Ben was in the process of playing "top" and Greg was "bottom." Both men immediately jumped out of bed and grabbed some towels and threw them around their waists. The towels did absolutely nothing to even slightly hide the hard-ons that each man was supporting.

"Well, we knew things were supposed to be a little different with the room arrangements that we agreed to, but this is really a little more different than what I expected." Tim stated.

"Hey guys, uhh, we sure didn't mean to interrupt anything. Uh, should we leave?" Chad asked.

"No, no!" Ben quickly replied. "God men we are sorry! We never meant to have you walk in on us doing this! We thought we had you two pretty well figured out as to when we should expect you to be here. I guess we kind of screwed up, didn't we? Really, we thought you guys were planning on being out till a lot later. We heard you talking about maybe having supper with some other people. So, we thought, well – anyway! We are sorry about this! We thought we had the room all to ourselves until a lot later!"

As Chad stood there with somewhat of a grin on his face, he inquired of the two rather embarrassed men. "Hey guys, as far as I'm concerned, what we walked in on is okay with me, but I've got to admit that I had no idea either one of you two were gay. Are you guys lovers? I mean, Greg, I thought you were a married guy!"

"No, no we're not! Yeah, right, Greg is married so please don't let this become a big deal, please!" Ben pleaded. "We only do this once in awhile when we get a chance, kind of like when guys go out of town and find themselves some woman to have sex with. Please guys, we sure never intended to have you guys find this out. Really we didn't! We thought we could do it and not let you guys know anything about it!"

Tim added to the statement of shock and concern. "Hey men, what you do with each other, is definitely none of our business. We're not going to make some big deal out of it, but I've got to admit, I've never seen two guys in bed together making out with each other, or actually in this case having actual sex with each other, so I've got to admit I'm kind of in a state of shock from seeing what I saw. Forgive me if I'm a little taken back by this, but what you do is up to you."

"So guys, tell me." Chad injected. "How often do you guys manage to do this? Greg, I have to assume that your wife is not aware of this, right?"

"No, hell no she's not aware! God if she ever found out, I'd be getting divorce papers before the day was over."

"Ben, you single, or is there a lady back home for you too?"

"No, I'm single. And I know, you are of course quickly assuming that I'm a gay, but I'm not sure if I am or not. Greg and I just like doing this whenever we get a chance, which is only probably maybe twice a year, so to us, it's just better than either one of us going out and finding some whore like most guys do. Guys, I'm sorry. We did not expect you two to be back so soon, really."

"Okay so we walked in at the wrong time. Stop apologizing for what happened. If either one of you had been up front with us, I really don't think Tim nor I, either one, would have made any kind of a fuss out of it. All you would have had to do is be up front with us, and then ask us to not come back to the room until some certain time. Come on Tim, let's go down to that BAR-B-Q place we saw and get some supper. Let's let the guys have their privacy. I'm sure they would have done the same thing for us, right guys?"

"Yeah we would have, but please don't leave just because of this! Guys, this is your room too. We can't have you leaving your room just because of what we do."

"No problem guys. Look, we will be out until at least nine o'clock. Okay? Don't feel bad about us leaving for awhile. Really guys, if we had been the ones in bed when you guys came in, I'm sure we would be glad if you two understood the situation and left for a while, so just forget we were here, and get back to your thing. We will see you after nine, okay? Okay Tim? Okay with you if we go get something to eat?"

As Tim and Chad headed out to give Ben and Greg some privacy time, they talked about the situation as they walked toward the Bar-B-Q restaurant they had seen earlier.

"So Tim, after the shock, what's your reaction? How you handling this?"

"Shocked like hell I guess, but I'm okay with it. They can do with each other whatever they want, I guess. I mean, I'm not their daddy, so I sure am not going to tell them they can't do that stuff. Guess maybe I'm a little surprised more to the age difference than anything else. Hey man, I'm smart enough to know stuff like that goes on all day long, everywhere, it's just that I've never been exposed to it though! But on the lighter side, did you see that fucking cock that Ben has got? I've got to admit that with us walking in on them like that, being shocked like I was, the whole idea that I noticed the hang of meat he has, kind of bothered me. I mean man, if it was ten feet long, I still should not have even noticed it."

"God man! Why not? Tim, you'll a normal human being. Of course you should have noticed it. Fact is I'm kind of glad that did happen so I could see what he was hanging. He was in just his briefs last night and he was showing so damn much in them, that I wondered just how big he was hung. Well man, got to admit, that's about the biggest one I've ever seen on some guy before."

"Well just how many dicks have you seen before? I've only seen the guys I used to shower with in high school gym and we were all just teenagers still growing – down there, in that department, and then of course just the guys that take a piss in the urinal beside me. So how many guys have you seen? Especially with a hard-on showing?"

"Oh, I don't know, maybe not that many, really."

"Wait a minute here Chad! I'm starting to get vibes here! I'm starting to feel that maybe you are not telling me everything, are you? This line of questioning is getting kind of bumpy for you isn't it?"

"Yes, yes it is. Let's just change the subject, okay?"

"No, no it's not okay! Chad, tell me! Have you had some experiences that I never knew about? Chad, you and I are very close friends. If there is something that I do not know, if you tell me, I'm not going to be upset. Chad, tell me, have you played around with guys before?"

"Yes, shit yes! Yes I have Tim, a few times!"

"See, now that didn't hurt now did it? Thank you! Thanks, I'm glad you told me. Now, question number two – who, oh and how often?"

"Hey man, just some guys. Nobody in particular, just some guys that I've found. Tim, you know – some of the customers that come in once in awhile and ask for me to wait on them. Some of those downtown lawyers and tax guys. Some of those guys! That's why they ask if I'm there or not. I'm not that good of a salesman, it's just that they know me from the bath house, and so they want me to make the commission."

"The bath house? Okay so now we are really getting somewhere. It's a little more than just a few guys, right? Maybe more like whenever you get horny. Right?"

"Oh shit Tim! Tim, you know as well as I do that I don't date one gal very long, do I? I have my girl friends, but pretty soon, they just do not interest me. Chad, I guess I must be BI! Yes, I like having sex with men! I've been doing that since I was about 17 or 18 maybe. Please Tim, let's just drop the subject. I don't want this stopping our friendship. Now you know, okay?"

"Yeah now I know, and Chad, I've got to tell you, now I like you better than I did five minutes ago.'

"What? What do you mean by that? Why would you say that?"

"Well simply because now I feel like we can be really, really honest with each other about anything. Chad, I mentioned your butt Sunday when we were checking into the room and I made comments about how you aren't running the stairs anymore, right?"

"Yeah."

"Well maybe there is something a little more about that comment than I really realized, even when I said it! Chad, I've admired that ass of yours ever since that first swim party. Chad, I've wondered ever since then if my watching that ass of yours was maybe something a little more than just seeing a solid ass. You were honest with me, I'm going to be honest with you. I've wanted to grab that ass and feel it ever since I've known you. What else I want to do, once I've got hold of it, I don't know, since I've never done anything like that! But Chad, since I now know that feeling it, would not offend you, will you let me grab your butt and feel it? I don't mean right now, not here, but when we are in the room? Chad, I've never touched some other guy's ass before, but being around you, I've wanted to so many times, and now, since we know each other a little better, I'm hoping maybe you will let me do that. I want to see just how solid it really is! Okay? The fact that you play with guys, is – in my mind, great! Well, great that is, if you will let me kind of do some playing with you. You are one great looking guy, and if any guy has ever thought about wanting to see what playing around with another guy is like, you would be the choice for choosing. Okay? Now you're not pissed at me are you?"

"No hell no, I'm not pissed at you! Why should I be pissed? Tim, I'm the guy that just admitted he likes to play with guys, you should be pissed at me!"

"Well, I'm not! Disappointed? You disappointed that I'm okay with this, and – really, kind of excited about it instead of being mad and pissed?"

"Tim, never in my wildest dreams did I think we would end up having this conversation, at this convention, let alone today. I will be honest and tell you that I have really wanted you to know about me for the whole time we have known each other, but I was just always afraid that you wouldn't like me if you knew that. Are you going to tell Jenny?"

"No! None of her business! Whenever you feel like the time is right, then you tell her. Okay?"

"Yeah – thanks man, thanks!"

"Okay, so now – the big question, before we go into the restaurant. So just when do I get to feel that ass of yours that I want to grab?"

"As far as I'm concerned, as soon as we get back to the room. Man, supper's going to be a little different tonight than usual, I can see. Tim, this is way too weird! I like it, the fact that what I told you is okay with you, and the fact that you want to feel my ass, but man, now we've got to go in there and act like – oh, everything is normal! My mind is really racing right now. Come on – let's go eat and talk about something else so nobody hears us talking about this! Okay?"

After eating some very calm and non-descript supper at the Bar-B-Q, and attempting to kill some extra time so that they did not get back to the room too early, Chad and Tim did leave the restaurant, and started walking back toward the hotel.

"Chad, I've got to tell you, it was rough sitting in there and trying to just eat instead of talking to you about what you've been doing. Tell me about doing it with a guy. I guess the more I think about it, the more I'm starting to realize that I truly have wanted to try it for a long time, but hey, being married and being a daddy, you just go the ole normal way. Chad, what's it like having sex with a guy?"

"God Tim! I'm not sure how to answer that! Man, what do I say? You know, I guess all I can say right now is, if you like the feel of a man's body, then having sex with that guy is a real turn on. It feels so different than having sex with a woman. With a guy, it's firm and solid. You can kind of handle him more roughly than a women. You can run your mouth along his muscles and feel his strength getting kind of transferred to you. When he grabs you and takes hold of you, you really know you are in bed with a real human being. Him grabbing and holding on feels so good. No woman can make it feel like that! I don't know Tim, it's so much different. The stuff you do with a guy, than with a woman, is so different too. I mean man, when was the last time a woman was able to fuck your ass? It's just all so different! It's man to man, 'solid and firm' to 'solid and firm'. No fluffy soft stuff. Tim, it's just different, great and different!"

"Oh shit man, fuck your ass? Oh God Chad, I never even thought about that being possible. Ben was fucking Greg when we walked in, wasn't he? He was on top of Greg's ass, and he sure as hell had a major hard-on, so I guess I must be right – Greg was getting it in the ass, wasn't he? Oh man, do you get fucked by guys? Have you ever been fucked by some guy?"

"Yeah – hell yes I do and yes I have! I guess since you know I play with guys, I might as well be open and honest with you. Yeah – I love to get it up the ass, and I might as well admit, the bigger the dick, the longer the dick, the stiffer the dick, the better I like it!"

"Like how big of a dick have you been fucked by? Like about how big was it?"

"Well, you saw Ben's right?"

"Yeah – but he hasn't fucked you – has he?"

"No, no! Not Ben, but from what I saw tonight, his and Stu's look like about the same size, and Stu's is the biggest one I've had."

"Stu? So who is Stu? Tell me who Stu is."

"Stu – he's the – hey if I tell you, never let him know I told you – okay?"

"Yeah okay! Stu, is he somebody I know?"

"Yeah – he's the lawyer that that's about maybe 30 or 32. Stands about five feet ten or eleven, real dark black hair and a mustache. Got the body every guy and every woman, including some old 95 year old woman would want. Hell, the way he's built, even some 95 year old man would want that! He bought that programmable massage chair last month."

"Oh shit Chad, you are kidding? That guy!? Wow, so he's hung like Ben is?"

"Yeah pretty much so."

"Damn man, that has got to look hot hangin' on the body that guy has got! What a package! Shit man – so how often do you and he play around?"

"Oh maybe once a month. Whenever his wife is out of town on business. She's some kind of a department head for the city, and she does these out of town trips every so often, and when she's gone, he gives me a call and asks if he can come over for awhile."

"Really, he's married and fucking around?"

"Oh hell yeah. Tim, there are a hell of a lot of married guys out there that get their kicks with other guys! And especially guys like Stu. He's so stuck on himself that he figures he can do anybody, anytime, anywhere he wants."

"But you play with him, anyway, right?"

"Yeah – guess maybe I fall into that group that wants that dick so badly that I'll put up with his attitude. Besides man, fucking my ass once in awhile, keeps him coming into the store and buying stuff. God – kind of makes it sound like I'm getting fucked by him just to make the commission, don't it?"

"So – his wife? I have to assume she is totally ignorant of this and his fucking around with guys? I mean, I assume he fucks other guys besides you, right?"

"Oh hell yeah! He's got a whole stable of us guys that he pokes. I know about three others that he does on a regular basis."

"His wife, she is totally unaware of this?"

"That I'm not too sure of, anymore! I don't know! I didn't think she knew anything at one time, but now I'm not too sure!"

"Why, why aren't you so sure anymore?"

"Shit man! She was out of town one week, and she called MY house looking for Stu. He wasn't there at that time, but why in the hell did she even know my name or my phone number? Stu just laughed it off later saying he had told here that if she needed him, and he did not answer at the house, to call my place. I never really got him to say yes or no, that he has told her what he does. So anyway, I figured, if she does know, and she doesn't care, why should I? Hey! I'm not going to screw up anything that makes him stop coming by my place and taking care of my ass, let me tell you! And besides, I figure that if she knows, she'll probably put up with it since she likes getting fucked by him as much as us guys do! She's not going to throw that dick out, that's for sure!"

"Well yeah. But, let me ask you Chad – getting something like that rammed up in your ass – don't that hurt?"

"Dry and too fast – yeah. Yeah, then it does. But with a little KY jelly, and just a little patience on both parts, then it's fucking heaven, let me tell you, fucking heaven!"

"So when did you last get fucked? How long's it been?"

Grinning and looking over toward Tim, Chad replied. "Well let's see. Today is Tuesday, right? Three days!"

"Three days? Three days?! Chad, you mean last Saturday?"

"Well, actually, Sunday morning! Before our flight Sunday! Hey man, I figured I'd be stuck here at the convention for five days, no chance to get any action, so I had Markie come over and spend the night with me Saturday night so that I could get it, and maybe get it out of my system for a few days. I sure as hell never expected this type of conversation happening here though." Then looking around to make sure nobody could see him, Chad rather turned toward Tim, reached down, pushed his rod back down his leg and said, "Tim, this talking is make me horny. My rod is standing up! Sorry man, but talking about doing it with other guys, just makes me get a hard-on."

Tim then grabbed his own crotch, and said, "I know man, I know. It is effecting me too, and I'm not even sure just what in the hell we are really talking about, but I know getting the chance to talk about this stuff with you is making me horny too. Chad, I've never been with a guy, but I've got to admit, this conversation is making me want to grab that ass of yours and maybe that thing on the front too."

"Tim, all I can say is, I hope like hell this talk and whatever is going to happen later does not ruin our friendship. I value our friendship too much to have it messed up."

"No Chad – do not worry! This will not ruin our friendship. Like I told you earlier, I like you better now than I did earlier. Now I feel like I really know you! Now Markie – this Markie guy, who is Markie? Never heard that name before."

"Oh Markie. Yeah little Markie! He's a bar back at the gay bar, My-Turn. Just barely old enough to be working behind the bar. We've known each other for about two years now. You know most gays are either a top, or a bottom. A top is the one that likes to do the fucking. A bottom is the one getting the fucking. Well Markie is definitely a top. Whenever I feel like my butt needs some attention, I can always count on Markie. Not hung like that lawyer Stu or that Ben, but hey man, action like crazy! Man, you've really got to be ready for that one to do you! Young and ambitious! He belongs out in the wilds somewhere. Anyway, last Saturday afternoon, I decided he was what I needed before the convention, and he was more than eager to accommodate me and my needs. Once late Saturday night after he got off of work, once early Sunday morning before we got up, and then he insisted on another one just before I headed for the airport. I figured I was well taken care of for the time at the convention."

"So you said he is the top, right?"

"Yeah."

"So I have to assume then, that you are a bottom, right?"

"Oh, well only part of the time. I'm what I guess you could call a flipper! Depends on what is going on, and who I'm with! With Markie, yeah I'm definitely a bottom, cause he is definitely the top. And same thing with Stu, but with him, maybe I'm bottom because that's where I want to be with him. Now there are some other guys that I am strictly top with, since they are exclusively bottoms. Me – hey whichever way, I'm not particular!"

"Man, I never imagined that you were doing this stuff. I guess you must have a gal on your arm often enough that I just never wondered. Chad, I wish you would have told me sooner, I really do!"

"Why, what difference would it have made? Why?"

As Tim looked at Chad, grinned and then looked down toward his own crotch, he answered, "Because of that! Chad, I've wanted to play with a guy for a long time now, but I just never had the chance or knew who to approach, and now that I know about you, I'm hoping to get some kind of a chance. Okay? I mean, I'm getting very straight forward here! I want to roll in the hay with you! Okay? I don't know if I want to be the top, or the bottom, but can we? You teach me, okay?"

Getting back to the hotel room, Chad and Tim lightly knocked on the door first, before opening it, to kind of warn Ben and Greg that they were about to come in, but they entered the room only to find Greg and Ben fully clothed, sitting at a side table reading some electronic sales literature that they had picked up at some of the booths at the convention.

"Well, this sure does look very primp and proper." Chad expressed as he closed the door.

"We are feeling pretty bad about what happened here earlier this evening," Greg said, "so we decided that we needed to act a little more respectful while we are around here and in the room. Once again, we are very sorry for doing what we did, and men, you can be sure it will not, and I do mean not, happen again."

"Like I said before guys, quit apologizing! Not that big of a deal, really!"

"Thanks man, and I mean it. How was dinner? Find something good?" Greg inquired.

"Yes I did, I definitely did!" Tim quickly entered. "Had a great dinner, didn't we Chad?"

With Tim now looking toward Chad with a very shitty assed grin on his face, Ben and Greg both looked at the other two men with a very quizzed expression on their faces.

Ben asked, "What do you mean? What is so funny about what you had for dinner?"

Grinning broadly, Tim replied. "Oh it's not what we had for dinner, it's just the before and the after, and I have to thank both of you for that!"

"What in the hell are you talking about? What do you mean thank us for what?" Greg emphatically asked.

Continuing to grin widely, Tim responded. "Well it's kind of like this! If we had not walked in on you two doing your "thing together," then this whole subject would never have come up, and I would never have found out – well while here in Vegas anyway, that Chad is into playing with guys too!"

Both Greg and Ben became very confused, and expressed it.

Ben asked, as he kept looking back and forth between Chad and Tim, "Chad is gay? Chad, are you gay? Is that what you are saying?"

"I don't know, I guess, hey I just don't know for sure. I admitted to Tim that I play around with guys, but then I date gals too, well sometimes."

"Yes – and the great thing is men – he has agreed to let me do some stuff, so to say, whatever I mean, like play around, I guess."

Greg looked at Tim, and asked. "Uhhh, Tim, do you play with guys? I'm confused here men, I getting real confused!"

"Greg, I've never played with a guy, but I've wanted to for a long time, and once I found out that Chad plays with guys, then I got real excited about maybe I've finally found somebody that I could do some stuff with. So anyway, I told him that for years I've wanted to grab that ass of his, and feel what it feels like, and he's told me I can. Haven't done it yet, but he's said I can!"

"Okay, so you are going to grab his ass, is that all? That's not too much playing around, is it? I mean, that's not going very far or doing very much if you are just going to grab his ass, is it?" Ben asked in a state of fluster and confusion.

Looking over toward Chad, and grinning broadly, Tim answered. "Yeah – that's right, but I guess we'll start with that and then see how things progress, right Chad?"

Greg looked over toward Ben and said, "Well guy, I kind of think this kind of sounds like you and me a few years ago, doesn't it? Sounds kind of familiar, don't it?"

"You know Greg, that's exactly what I was just standing here thinking. Sure does sound familiar!"

"Hey guys what are you saying?" Tim asked. "You mean your first time with each other? How did you two ever get together the first time?"

"Totally by accident, totally by accident!" Greg answered. "We lived, well still do live in the same neighborhood. I and my family have a house there, and Ben lives in an apartment, kind of around the corner. There's a community swimming pool what everybody around there uses. Well anyway, I had seen Ben at the pool a number of times that summer, and every time I saw him, I kept thinking how hot of a body he had, and the more I saw him, the more I kept thinking about how I thought I'd like to play with him, or let him play with me, or anyway, something that I really did not know for sure what. And of course, he wore hardly any trunks at all. Every time I saw him, I kept thinking that whatever he had in the crotch of those trunks, it was going to fall out pretty soon, 'cause I could tell it was too damn big for being in the trunks he had on."

With that comment, Tim and Chad both looked down toward Ben's crotch and grinned. Chad grinned, and in addition, licked his lips. Ben saw what had happened, and grinned broadly as he looked at Chad and Tim.

"Anyway, all I could ever do is just look and wonder what it would be like. I'd never been with a guy before, so it was all just wondering and just imagining. Then, one night I discovered that I had left a towel and some sun glasses at the pool. When I discovered that, it was getting late and I wasn't sure the pool would still be open so that I could get them, but I ran back over to the pool to see if it was still open. It looked dark, but when I tried the gate, it opened, so I thought, well I'll just go in and see if they are still laying there beside the chair. I did not know at that time that Ben, as I later found out his name was, that he worked at the pool part time. All I can say is, he rather failed to lock the outside gate, before he took that hot little hunk of a guy named Sammy into the equipment area and let Sammy get that dick of his, pushed up in his ass. I saw what was happening, and I froze. I watched Ben fuck little Sammy for probably five minutes before I finally, and I do mean in total desperation, walked over toward them and let them know I was there and was watching. Freaked Ben out, totally! I kept telling him it was no big deal! Little Sammy, as Ben always called him, grabbed his trunks and after pulling them on, as fast as he could, he ran! I finally got Ben to calm down enough so that I could tell him how I had been admiring him all summer long whenever I saw him, and I told him that I had been wanting to do something with him ever since I first saw him earlier that summer. Then I just blurted out and asked him if we could have some sex together."

As Chad was rubbing his own crotch, he exclaimed, "Oh shit man, oh shit! God, this is too fucking hot to believe! What in the hell did you do then? Well, I guess something good must have happened. It sure looked to me like you still get fucked by him, right?"

"He was, of course, afraid that I'd say something to the people that ran the pool, so I told him that if he'd let me play with him, then I'd keep my mouth shut! Boy! Does that sound like blackmail? So, anyway, he gave me my first blow job there in the equipment room that night. That was after I suggested he go lock the gate though. We made some arrangements for me to visit his apartment the next night, since he didn't have to be at the pool that night, and that was my first real gay session. And damn man, it was good! Have you guys seen the dick on this guy?"

"But wait a minute here. I'm confused!" Chad said. "Then you two just saw each other at the pool, right? But now you work together, right?"

"Oh yeah! He was working two part time jobs, the pool being one of them, and so when the store needed a new guy on the sales floor, I told him to come in and apply, but just don't let anybody know that we knew each other. So, of course, since I was the hiring manager, I sure did like his application, and of course he interviewed "very well," so I decided he was the man to hire. For God sake men, don't ever let anybody in our company know what I have told you! Or my wife for that matter either! You guys now know more about Ben and I, and how we met, and of course what we do together, than anybody else! For God sake, keep it a secret!"

"Hey we will man, definitely we will! Got to remember men, I've got the wife and family back home too, but before I go home, I will have finally found out what playing with a guy, and I will admit – if I may, a very hot guy, is like."

Looking over toward Ben, Greg then said. "You know what man, I think it is time that you and I maybe went down to that cocktail lounge that we found, and maybe let these two guys have the room all to themselves, for awhile, don't you think?"

"Yes, I definitely agree! Let me hit the bathroom for a minute, and I'll be ready."

Ben came back out of the bathroom, looked at Chad and told him, "Hey man, left something on the counter in there for you. See you guys later. Let's say, not before eleven, okay?"

"Yeah thanks men, thanks!" Chad and Tim both expressed as Greg and Ben left the room.

With a very quizzed expression on his face, Tim asked, as he looked at Chad, and then headed for the bathroom, "Left something on the counter for you? What did Ben mean by that?"

Chapter Three:
Then You Can Grab It

"Oh! Chad, he left a tube of sexual lubricant. I assume that means he figures somebody is going to get it up in the ass, right?"

Laughing, Chad stuck his head in the bathroom door and replied, "Well, I guess so. Or at least he figured that since he had some here in the room, that he'd at least make it available so that if we did need it, we could use it. It's just you and me in here man, I kind of guess the time is getting close for you to grab my ass like you've been saying you want to do, isn't it?"

"Oh God yes! Yeah, I guess it is. Come here and let me put my hands on it. Let me grab it."

Right then Chad turned away from the bathroom door and answered back, "Hey not so fast man, not so fast! Come out here and get stripped down. We're going to take a shower together, and then when it is good and soapy, then you can grab it, okay?"

"Oh okay, if that's what you want. Taking a shower with you is even a hell of a lot more than I was asking for. Chad, this is getting really kind of exciting for me. I thought I was just going to get to grab your butt to see how tight and solid it is, but hey, if you want to, I sure am not going to say no! Hell, not the way I'm feeling right now anyway!"

Chad and Tim started stripping all of their clothes off, and since Chad was totally naked first, he returned to the bathroom and got in the shower and started to adjust the water temperature. Tim finished getting undressed and went into the bathroom.

Looking down at his now completely firm and straight hard-on, standing proudly out in front of himself, Tim said, "Oh Chad, shit man! This is getting me hotter than I have been in a hell of a long time."

Chad looked over at him as Tim entered the bathroom and after taking a quick second look, he said, "Wow! Shit man! Oh my God man, I never expected to see that much coming out of those pants! Shit man! Tim, I sure as the hell never knew you were hung like that! Shit man you're hung like a horse! Crap man – we should have been doing something together a long time ago. Damn man! You've got one hell of a donger on you! Come on man, get in this shower! Let me get my hands on that damn thing!"

With Tim being quite nervous about doing even the ass grabbing for his first time, and now Chad's anxiety, after seeing what Tim had been hiding from him for so long, both circumstances were making a little more steam in the shower than what the water was.

"Shit man! You made comments about Ben's dick and how big it is. God Tim! Look at what in the hell is hanging on you! God man, I think you are bigger than Ben is. Maybe now I know why you were asking about getting it up the ass with a big dick and how big of a dick I've taken up my ass before. I don't know if you realize it or not, but you were really wondering if maybe I could take that damn big thing of yours up my butt, weren't you? Shit man! I know damn well that I'm going to get fucked by that one, and then when somebody asks me how big of a dick I've taken, it's going to be yours that I remember. God man! I need to feel you up in me. All the way up in me!"

With Chad being aged 26 and being the definite athletic, with the definite athlete's body, he just normally felt that he probably did have the more "manly body" compared to Tim, but all of a sudden his assumptions were becoming a total myth. As Tim, 6 foot-1, stood there fully bare, and showing another man, more skin than he had ever shown before, especially since one particular part of it was now stretched to its maximum, he was letting Chad realize that the older guy, even though he was only three years older, definitely was no slouch in the body arena. His nine and a half to ten inch long dick, which looked like it probably measured about five to five and a half inches around, definitely reminded Chad of a dildo he saw hanging on display in a book store novelty shop a few months ago. He had admired that fake dick, and he had wanted to see what it felt like stuck up in his butt, but since he did not end up buying it, he never found out what it felt like. But he was now definitely certain that if he did not screw up this session, tonight, too badly, he would shortly be getting the real thing stuck up in there for him and his inners to enjoy!

"Come in here man, come in here! I want to put my hand on that thing! God Tim, what a fucking dick you've got! I cannot believe that for as long as I have known you that I never had any hint of an idea that you had this much cock on you. Man, I wish I had known that! Man, you've been wanting to grab my ass and all I can tell you right now is I wish like hell I had known about that thing a long time ago – cause you could have been grabbing my ass while you're sticking that thing up in me! Tim, you're going to fuck my ass before this night is over! Fuck man, what a fucking dick you've got! Seriously Tim, if I had known you were hung that way, I would have been up front and honest with you about my gay ways, a long time ago, just so I could have found out if you'd fuck me or not! Shit man, I need that!"

Tim stepped into the shower, and it had immediately become obvious that Tim's desire to grab a handful of Chad's ass was now definitely the lesser of the main aims of things that were now happening.

"Now I understand why in the hell you always wear those baggy beach pants at the company pool parties. Shit man, I just figured you were kind of shy or maybe just didn't like tight trunks, but crap man, now I know! With a dick like that you probably can't hardly wear a pair of Speedos or some tight trunks, can you? Well – I mean, yeah I know you can wear them, but when you do, it really shows all of you don't it?"

"Yeah, it does. I own one pair of tight swim trunks, but I never wear them. I did once and I felt like everybody all afternoon long were kind of just walking past me so they could see my crotch. Maybe I was just self-conscious, but really I just felt like everybody was looking at me, so I never wore them again!"

"Shit man, I'd love to see them on you! I'll bet that's hot looking. Hey Tim, I want you to bring them over to my place someday and put them on for me. I want to see what that looks like, okay? I want to see that dick all squeezed up in them, and then I want to put my face on it and just lick it through the fabric of those trunks. I want to just mouth and tongue your crotch with that dick inside. Can I do that?"

"Yeah – if you want! Sure I'll do that! It's been years since I've put them on, but I'm sure I know where they are, so hell yeah, if you want to see it, I'll do it!"

As Tim and Chad stood in the shower stall, Chad had definite trouble of trying to look at anything else, other than Tim's very big surprise that still had Chad all shook up.

As Tim stepped in the shower, Chad immediately reached out and took hold of Tim's stiff rod. Chad licked his lips some, and as he grabbed the rod, he laid his head on Tim's chest and started stroking Tim's cock.

"Oh Tim! Tim this, this is so unbelievable! This is great! You've never had some other guy grab it like this before?"

"No, I sure haven't Chad and I will tell you it feels good. I never thought about what it could feel like if some guy had hold of it and was squeezing it like you are. Oh man, you are really making it hard and stiff. That feels so good! Oh Chad I never expected to feel something like this! Oh man, squeeze it tight and hard!"

Chad was mesmerized with the hunk of meat that he was now handling and was sliding the un-cut foreskin back and forth as far as he could get it to slide.

"Oh Tim, I love this man, I love this!"

Suddenly without warning, Chad dropped to his knees and without fanfare, he immediately took the first half of Tim's cock into his mouth.

"Oh my God – oh man, oh shit man – oh God!! Oh Chad that feels so fucking good man! Oh shit man I had no idea you were going to do that! Oh Chad suck on me – suck on me, suck on me, suck on me!!"

Tim's desire of just feeling Chad's ass had become a total non-issue. Without any discussion or forewarning that it was going to happen, Tim was realizing that he now, stood there with more than half of his dick stuck down in the mouth of his friend and co-worker. Even though Chad had already told Tim that he was "into" guys, Tim never pondered the idea that maybe Chad would even think about chewing and sucking on his dick. He had rather unconsciously figured that Chad's "guy playing around" would still be only with other guys, guys that Tim did not know, and certainly not with him. The excitement that he was now standing there, with his hands on Chad's head, and with his dick firmly planted into Chad's face, he realized that he was now experiencing more sexual anxiety than he had ever experienced in his entire life. He had never had his dick stuck into some guy's face before, and now he was standing there with his dick firmly planted in not just a guy's mouth, but it was Chad's mouth! His closest friend. A man he had known for years and had spent a lot of time with, but never, never any time like this!

"Oh Chad I thought the first time with a girl was exciting and hot but man, this is way over the top!! Oh Chad I love this, I love this! Oh suck on it please, suck on me! Oh man, oh man! I had no idea that you were gonna put my dick in your mouth and suck on it. Oh grab my nuts please, oh yeah grab 'em man, grab 'em and squeeze 'em – squeeze 'em! Oh man I cannot believe this is happening, I cannot! Oh Chad, suck it man, suck it! Oh yeah, oh yeah, oh suck the head off of it man, suck it hard – suck it hard!"

As he was now pleading for Chad to suck him stronger, Tim was into the natural reactions of strongly grabbing hold of Chad's head and forcing it up against his gut as tightly as possible so that Chad was almost forced to swallow the entire dick. For more than ten or maybe fifteen minutes, Chad took Tim's big rod and sucked on it, chewed on it and enjoyed each and every square inch of it to his greatest of joy.

As he sucked on it and chew on it, Chad did reach up and grab a hold of Tim's bag of balls and manipulated them around and around in his hand, and softly squeezed 'em so that Tim did know that his nuts were being played with.

All of a sudden Chad stood up, turned the water off, opened the shower door and told Tim that they needed to get into the bedroom so that he could get fucked by that enormous dick.

"Come on Tim, I gotta get that thing up in my ass and let you shoot off and cum up in there. Once I saw that thing, I immediately knew I needed to get that thing rammed up in my butt, and so we gotta go do it. I want that up in my ass! I gotta have it in my ass, I gotta! Oh man, it's gonna feel like I got a baseball bat up in there!"

"Oh shit man, I can't believe I'm actually gonna fuck your ass Chad. I can't believe it! Oh man, I've just wanted to grab it for so long now, and now you're really gonna let me fuck it? Really, I'm gonna fuck it?"

"Hell man, I'm not gonna let you fuck it, I fucking demanding that you fuck it! You ain't got any choice about it, I gotta have that big think stuck up in my ass and you gotta fuck me good with it! Come on man, fuck me, and fuck me hard!"

They both left the shower, toweled off some and hit the bed.

Tim grabbed the lube that Ben had left behind for them, he smeared some on his dick, and some on Chad's ass. After expressing how exciting it was and how great his ass felt with his hand sliding up in-between Chad's ass checks – the very same ass he's had been wanting to grab for years now

– he wiped the excess grease off of his hand. He moved up close to Chad's ass, he took ahold of his own dick, he directed it toward Chad's asshole and slid it up between Chad's ass cheeks. Tim hugged Chad around the waist with his right hand, and guided his dick with his left hand. He found the hole.

"Yeah man! Yeah, slow now! Go slow! I've got to get my ass opened up some before you ram that damn big thing up in me all the way! I gotta get my ass opened up some. I gotta make sure I can take this! Go in me real slow, man, real slow! I gotta get my ass opened some before you push that whole damn thing up in there! Go slow."

"Yeah, I will. I will. Can you feel the tip of my dick?"

"Hell yes man, hell yes! Yeah, Tim I can! You've got it right at my asshole. Move toward me a little more but just be slow! Yeah man! Yeah, move toward me and keep your dick aimed right at my hole, right where it is now!"

Tim squeezed Chad's waist as he pulled himself up closer to Chad, and thrust his dick forward so that it would enter Chad's ass. It slid in! Chad jerked and yelled, "Ouch! Oh man! Oh God man! Oh Tim, don't move! Oh Tim! When you pushed it in me, it kinda hurt! I guess maybe I wasn't quite ready for it. Just lie there for a moment! It doesn't hurt anymore, but let me just try and get used to having something that fucking big stuck up in me. That's one fucking big cock! That's bigger than anything I've had up in there for a long time."

Then Chad laughed and added, "Well man, I guess you can say you just fucked your first guy's ass, can't you?"

Tim grabbed ahold of Chad with both hands wrapped around his body and asked, "Hey, man! You okay? Are you alright?"

"Yeah, I'm okay now, but for a second there, it did kinda hurt. But now it's feeling pretty good up in there. Push up against me a little more and let me take some more of it. I want it all up in there!"

Tim pulled Chad's body up against his own, and pushed his dick in a little more.

"Yeah Tim, that feels good! Tim, see if you can push more of it in me."

Tim, once again, pushed his rod up against Chad's ass and let more dick enter into Chad's body. Chad did not complain or say to stop, so Tim continued to push, and shortly he discovered that he had all of his dick up and in Chad's ass.

"Chad! You've got all of me up inside of you now! How is that feeling? Is it okay? You didn't tell me to stop, so I kept pushing, and now it's all up in you. You okay? How does your ass feel?"

Slightly turning and twisting his head, partly holding it up and partly letting it lay down on the bed, Chad moaned, "Oh shit man! Oh God Tim! Oh Tim – once that initial pain passed, man, ever since then, this has been great! I cannot believe I have your whole damn dick up inside of me! God man! All we were supposed to do was let you grab my ass and then I saw that enormous cock of yours, and everything changed! Man – oh man! Tim, we sure, as hell, went way past just the grabbing my ass. Your dick up in me feels great, just fucking great! I feel like I've got an eighteen wheeler up in me, and it's got its motor running full force !"

"Yeah Chad, we sure as hell did man, but Chad I don't have one regret about it! Well my one regret is that I wish that we could have been doing this for a long time now, but yeah, I'm the married guy and I was real afraid of letting you know that I wanted to feel that ass of yours! Sex with you, and fucking you is great! I'm really having myself one hell of a great time! I've never done this before, but I love what we're doing. This is so much more exciting than I ever thought sex could be! Man, this is it! Chad, this is what really being a man is! Doing sex, in a big strong, rough, manly way, I love it!"

"Tim that damn big pole of yours feels so fucking good up in there! Hey – kind of move it around some. Kind of jerk it back and forth and let me feel it. Oh Tim, I know already, I love to have a big dick in my ass, and yours is a big one! Fuck me and shoot off up in there guy! I wanna feel you fuck the hell out of me now that I've got all of it up in there, and I wanna feel you shoot off! Do it man, fuck me hard! You just said you like doing sex, in a big strong, rough, manly way – so do it! Fuck me as rough as you want to man, cause man, it's feeling great, fucking great! Fuck me like you are some big wild horny animal out in the rough!"

For the rest of their private time available, Tim was in Chad's ass and succeeded in coming in his ass, a total of three times. Every time Tim thought maybe they should stop, Chad told him to, "Just keep fucking me man, keep fucking! If those guys come back before we get done, so be it. We walked in on them earlier today, and so let 'em walk in on us! We're making up for a lot of lost time, and right now I know what the most important thing is, that I found out about while in Vegas, and it has nothing to do with electronics. It has everything to do with my co-worker, my hung like a horse co-worker, and once we get back home – he will be my favorite co-worker and my favorite sex mate! When I call you 'Stud,' remember I've got one hell of a good reason to call you that! I maybe never really understood the big true reasons of why big guys were called 'Stud,' but after getting my ass rammed with that big thing, now I agree totally! I feel like that is a fucking horse back there, using my ass. Oh thank goodness for an electronics convention, and thank goodness for one hotel that just was not quite put all back together – quit yet! Having roommates that you really do not know anything about, can be a good thing – a really good thing! Funny things can happen! It sure paid off for us! Keep fucking me man – keep fucking me! I gotta have you up in me for as long as I can, clear up till the time we gotta go home. When Ben and Greg get back, then maybe we can stop long enough to tell them how fucking glad we are that we walked in on them at the 'wrong' time."

INTER-RELATIONSHIP TRAINING MEETING

Chapter One:
Jay, You'll Learn To!

"Oh shit!"

"Huh, what's the matter?"

"Huh, somebody just came in."

"Oh shit! That gonna be a problem?"

"No, just lay there! We'll just see what happens."

Jay was on the bed, on the back of, and in the ass of, some guy, who's name he did not even know, when Darrell walked into the cabin and started past the bedroom door, but then abruptly stopped, and with his mouth hanging wide open, he asked. "Hey what in the hell is going on in here?"

Jay looked back over his shoulder and replied, "Huh, kind of hard to explain right now, but anyway, he asked and I decided to see what it was like. I thought you weren't gonna be back so soon."

"Who is he? What's going on? Where'd he come from?"

As Jay stopped his pumping and humping actions, but none the less, kept his meat rod well buried in the guy's ass, he told Darrell, "Darrell, gotta be honest with you and tell you I don't even know his name. He was on one beach chair and I was laying on the one beside him, we talked for awhile, and when I got up to go to the beach shower to rinse off, he followed me. While we showered, he kind of let me know he was interested and finally told me, 'That looks pretty good,' as he was looking down at my crotch. Then without saying anything else, he kept rubbing his ass, letting me kind of know he wanted me to do something. He kept looking at my basket and then rubbing his ass, and I finally put two and two together and decided he was trying to see if I was smart enough to figure out he wanted us to do something. So I finally asked if he was trying to tell me he wanted fucked, and he said 'Yes.' Shocked the hell out of me, but I figured hell, he's got the balls to say so – so here we are!"

"Jay, I'm really confused here! Jay, you're not gay are you? You're married! Jay, what in the hell is going on? I'm really confused!"

"Hey Darrell, like the guy said in class yesterday – have a little more of an open mind when being with other people and it might be easier to get to know them and understand them. So, hey! I thought, what better of a way to try that out! I know I sure would never have approached some guy for something like this, but hey – he did, and right now I'm pretty glad he had the guts to do it! True, I've never done anything with another guy before, but he told me he wanted me to fuck him, and I decided, why not! I figured it's his ass not mine, so I figured this just might be a once in a lifetime opportunity, and I decided to go for it! Besides that, look at him. I figured if you're gonna fuck some guy's ass, make sure he's a hunk! He sure don't look like what some gay guy is supposed to look like does he? Darrell, it's feeling pretty damn good too!"

Looking down at the man, the rather hunky man laying on the bed, with Jay's cock firmly planted up in his ass, Darrell asked, "Huh, who are you? You got a name?"

Looking back toward Darrell, the man replied. "Hi, I'm Stan, short for Stanley. I sure hope this ain't causing any problems for you! He told me nobody was gonna be here, so we really didn't expect anybody to come in. Should I leave?"

"No – no don't leave. Yeah, I didn't expect that meeting to be this short either, and yeah, I didn't expect to be back till about noon, and I sure as hell didn't expect to come walking in on some gay sex session, so maybe I'm the one that needs to leave."

"No Darrell, don't leave!" Jay quickly stated. "Hey give me a minute with him, and we'll be done. I'm not asking for the time for him, I'm the one that needs it now! I'm really getting into this, and I've got to get my rocks off now that I've been fucking this ass. This is not really a gay sex session.

I just decided to take an opportunity when all of a sudden it presented itself. I've never done this before, and I've gotta admit, I'm kind of finding it to be something rather different, and yeah, kind of a new and different way to start understanding other kinds of people! We're here trying to learn how to work with other types of people, and hell, maybe this guy was planted here to see how some guy would take it if he was approached. Anyway, I'm really finding out, that if you do have more of an open mind, things can work out for the good. Yeah, I gotta admit – agreeing to fuck some guy's ass, somebody you don't even know, is really being very open minded, but hey, this time it sure is working out OK! Do whatever you want, but if you wanna do something kind of on the different side, get undressed and get ready to fuck him. Go for something new and exciting! I'm sure he wouldn't mind. Hey, Stan, can he fuck you too, if he wants?"

"Hell yes he can! Fact is I hope he will! Both of you guys are pretty damn hot, and since I don't have any of my university football players here with me, I could enjoy both of you guys doing me. I'm here for the whole week too, and I need some action!"

"Football players? You get fucked by university football players?"

Stan calmly just shook his head a slight, "Yes."

"Yeah Darrell – he told me over on the beach he's a defensive coordinator at a State University. Now that I kind of think about it, I think maybe he told me that so I'd take notice of his body! He was probably trying to get me all hot and bothered for him, even before we showered down."

Then leaning over and looking at his bed partner he asked, "Is that why you told me about you being a coach? You wanted me to notice all your muscles, didn't you?"

Jay did not receive any verbal response, only the sight of one big grin on Stan's face. That told the story!

Looking back at Darrell, Jay continued, "He didn't tell me which state, I didn't ask, and of course at that time he sure didn't tell me his guys fuck his ass, but I did know he was a coach. We didn't talk about sex over on the beach! That didn't happen till we were showering, and hell man, I still had my trunks on! It's an outside shower!"

Jay and Darrell were just two of a group of six that were at the South Carolina beach resort for the week, attending an Inter-Relationship Training Meeting. They were both managers for a large computer company, and this was a company paid training session. Designed to be a rather business session, training session, and a reward week, away from the office. The six men were using two cabins, side-by-side, with three men staying in each cabin. Jay, Darrell and Tom were rooming together. The other cabin had Sidney, Robert, and James.

Jay was married, aged forty-five with two college aged daughters. Not an athletically outstanding body, but certainly nothing that a horny gay guy would turn down, especially if he found out the guy wanted to throw his legs up in the air, and then throw a stiff cock into his nice warm ass. Obviously hot enough for Stan, since he had managed to gather Jay up off of the beach, and end up getting Jay's cock slammed up into his ass. And that was before either man even knew the other man's name.

Darrell was also married, aged thirty-four and had a young son and a young daughter. A young son, a young daughter and one hell of a hot body! As Stan laid there on the bed, with Jay calmly explaining the situation – of just why Stan was there, and just how Stan happened to be getting fucked by Jay, Stan prayed a big "Yes" when Jay suggested that perhaps Darrell might want to, "get undressed and get ready to fuck him!"

Darrell listened rather closely when it was mentioned that Stan was a defensive coordinator for a state university football team, since he had played some football back in his high school and university days. Having recently moved from across country to take on the promotion as a department manager, he knew immediately he did not know who any of the local coaches were, at any of the colleges or universities in that part of the country. But, remembering back to his football days, he found this quite interesting and quite fascinating! Football players fucking one of the coaches!? That made him seriously run the list of co-players he had played football with, wondering if any of them had used the ole asshole of one of his former coaches. Or, even more fascinating, did any of his coaches use the ole asshole of some of the players? A player and a coach having sex together!? That just never happened to occur to him as an event of any possible reality. A player and a coach!? Gay guys!? Football players and football coaches!? Gay!? Far too hard to even ponder, and yet here was a defensive coordinator, for a state university, laying there, legs spread wide open, getting his ass fucked. And fucked by one of Darrell's own co-workers! And not a guy of university age, either! Darrell realized very quickly that this week was having some very serious relationship learning associated with it, but the more intensive learning was not happening in the classroom, it was happening right there in the bedroom! 'My straight co-worker, is actually fucking the ass of some guy, that nobody in their right mind could ever think of as being gay, or even bi! No coach ever plays with other guys, do they!? Impossible! Coaches just are not gay guys! Are they!?'

Looking up at Darrell, Stan asked, "Ever fucked some guy's ass before?"

"No – no I haven't. I know guys do that, but I sure didn't know that university football coaches do it! Jay, you ever fucked some guy before?"

"No Darrell, no I haven't. But, like that guy said yesterday – have a little more of an open mind and it's easier to get to know other people. Darrell, I'm serious, you ought to try it! I'm sure you're not gonna tell anyone I fucked him, and I sure as the hell am not gonna tell anyone if you do, so if you wanna, I'm sure he'll let you! Yeah, it's different, but it's feeling pretty damn good! I'm sure he'll let you, won't you Stan?"

"Hell yes! I've already said I'm willing! Come on man, do me! Fuck me! Find out for yourself what it's like to fuck a guy's ass, for a change!"

As Darrell continued to stand there and ponder the situation, Jay resumed his fucking, realizing that Darrell was fully aware of the entire situation, and with everything out in the open, there certainly was no reason to stop now. He decided that maybe the best way to get Darrell to agree to join in, was to just let him stand there and watch Stan get fucked – and the harder, the better! He truly started pounding Stan's ass, good and strong!

"Oh yeah man, oh yeah! Oh that feels so good! Yeah pound me – pound me real hard! Hey, I like this, keep it up!"

Jay continued his fucking action in Stan's ass as he slowly slid his tongue up and down the back of Stan's massive, strong, muscular back, and ever so slightly would stop every so often, and slightly take a slight, light, bite of Stan's back skin.

"Oh yeah, oh yeah! I like that! Hey, I got a feeling I ain't the first guy you've ever laid on top of am I? You know how to treat a guy! Yeah man, yeah keep it up!"

"No Stan. Wrong! You are the first guy I've ever laid on top of, and you sure as hell are the first guy I've ever stuck my cock up in! Right now though, I'm gonna tell you, I'm sure not sorry I'm doing this! I've always wondered just why the gay guys did this, but shit man, now I know! This is good! Fact is this is great! Hey man, OK if I cum up in your butt? I feel like I'm getting pretty close to letting some cum fly and I'd kind of like to keep pumping on you while I let it go! OK? I'm getting close man, I'm getting close!"

"Yeah man, yeah! I wanna feel it hit the inside of me! Come on, let me have it, let me have it!"

As Stan was telling Jay to unload up in his ass, he kept an eye on Darrell, and although he was sure Darrell simply was not aware of it, Darrell was definitely rubbing his own crotch as he watched Jay work himself up into a major climax, and his crotch was starting to show some definite additional size – from what it was when he just happened in on the sex scene.

"Oh my God! Oh my God, man! I'm cumin – I'm cummmmmmin!" Jay threw his body into Stan's ass just as hard and as firmly as he possibly could. He grabbed Stan's chest and hugged it with all he could – as he let fly, his first ever juices that were going to be planted up in some other man's ass!

As he completely and totally collapsed on top of Stan's body, he slowly and softly let out, "Oh man, that was great! That was great! I have never had sex that was that great! Darrell, come fuck this guy! Really man, I kid you not! You'll be glad you did. I'm serious man, fucking a solid firm muscle filled ass like that is absolutely out of this world!"

Stan looked over toward Darrell, watched him rub his crotch, actually watched as Darrell unknowingly presented the outline of his dick's head, through his Dockers, and Stan pleaded, "Come on man, I need you! I'm just getting warmed up here! Your buddy got me going and now I need some more dick, do me, OK? Do me!"

With that statement, Darrell did, and almost as if he did not really know what he was doing, started to unbuckle his belt, and loosen his pants.

"Yeah please, please!" Stan again begged. "You'll be glad! I promise!"

"Looking at Jay, then looking at Stan, who did still have Jay's rod up in his ass, Darrell said, "God guys! Watching and listening to you two guys has got me so fucking hot, I gotta do it! God almighty, I never thought I'd ever be fucking some guy's ass, but man, I've got to now, after watching you guys go at it! Damn man, I'm ready to do it!"

As Darrell started removing his clothes, Stan happily said, "Yeah man, yeah! You'll be glad!"

Jay pulled out of Stan's ass and asked, "Should we put some more KY up in your ass, or you think you've still got enough left up in there from me?"

Stan turned looked at Jay and said, "Hey man you are one good fucker! I still think you must have fucked some other guys before! Damn man, you know how! You know how to make a man's ass happy! I hope like hell you and I can do that again before we all have to leave here! Huh – oh – the KY! Hey, just put some on the tip of his dick so it slides nice an smooth, but I think I've already got enough up in me. Wow—look at the honker on that man! Shit man, did you know he was so fucking well hung?"

Hearing Stan's remark of exclamation, Jay turned to see what Stan was expounding about.

"Oh holy shit!" Jay strongly stated as he took the first look at Darrell's nine and a half or ten incher, sticking straight out! "Holy shit man, where in the hell did you get that thing? My God Darrell – you are hung like a fucking horse! God Stan, now I'm glad I got to you before he did or you would never have felt mine up in you!"

"No – not true Jay! Even after getting poked with a big one like that, a smaller one still feels great! Our asshole slams back shut after you pull a dick out, so whatever size the next one is, it still feels great. Hey man, you're gonna have to get it up the ass sometime so you will find out being the taker is just as much fun as being the giver! I like to be the fucker part of the time too, but today I just felt like I really needed it slammed to me. And now, seeing what he has got hanging there, I know damn well I will know I got it. Come on big boy, get on me, but go slow! My ass can take it, and once it's up in there, I'll be yelling for more, but we gotta take one that fucking big, pretty slow going in! I don't wanna take a ripped and torn up asshole back home to my team boys! They'd be pissed if they couldn't get to it right away!"

Watching Darrell get into position so that he could do his first male fucking, and listening to Stan talking about his football player, sex players, Jay asked, "Stan, just how may football boys you have? I mean for sex! How many are into the gay sex?"

"Oh wait a minute – wait a minute. Oh man, oh let me get him started in me first. Oh man, oh shit I can really feel that! Oh my God my ass feels so full! Oh yeah, now push-push! Yeah man-yeah-go all the way-all the way! Oh God that is great! Oh shit what an ass full! Hey, how you doing? Like it? Hey guy, you've got your dick, that fucking railroad car of a dick, up in my ass! How's it feeling to you? You like it?"

"Oh shit yes, yeah I like it! Hell yes! Damn man your ass is so fucking tight! Oh man, this is good! Oh God I'm glad I came back when I did! Oh shit man, now I know why there's gay guys! Damn man, wish like hell someone would have made me to this to them years ago! Oh shit Jay, this is hot!"

"Hey man, you're in me, you're in me all the way, right? Now fuck the hell out of me! Pump me, slam my ass! Yeah man, yeah! Pound me to a fucking pulp! Make me know what I've got up in there! Beat my ass, beat it!"

"Oh shit man, if he pounds you any harder, he's gonna rip you in two! Stan, he is pounding the hell out of you! You OK?"

"Oh fucking yeah, I'm OK! I'm more than OK right now! Oh shit man, I'm getting fucked, and I do mean fucked! Damn man you guys really know how to do a guy! Whoa, maybe I need to trade my football boys in on some older guys! Damn man, both of you guys are better on me than any of my football boys are! Oh – forgot – you asked about how many guys I've got! I think – oh, wait a minute – yeah, pound it man – pound it – damn man that is so fucking good – oh God, I'm sorry – I've got six guys right now. I try to keep it spread out through all the different ages so I don't go and loose too many all in one year. Like I'm gonna lose two seniors this year! And damn, that Billy is so fucking good too! God I love for him to slam my ass! That's one boy I make stay late after practice a lot! He's a black boy, hung like a fucking sausage, but I don't think he's as big as the one I've got rammed up in me right now! God oh God man! This one that's fucking me now, what's his name Darrell – he is fucking big! I feel like I know what it's like to get fucked by a horse now!"

"Yeah, I gotta agree with that! He just joined our office recently, so of course I had no idea he was hung like that! Gotta admit, the way you are enjoying it though, kind of makes a guy wonder if maybe the rest of us are all missing out on something here!"

Stan was looking at Jay and he grinned! He thought he knew what Jay was saying, even though Jay might not have realized just what he was really meaning.

Even though Darrell was doing his best at trying to pulverize Stan's body with his humping and bumping back in his ass area, he heard the remark and also grinned a wide, smiling grin.

Looking now at Darrell, Jay asked, "So what you grinning about all of a sudden?"

"You do realize you just admitted that maybe you could get into getting fucked too, right? That's what you just said. You decided that maybe "the rest of us,' meaning you – are missing out on something. To me, that sounds like maybe you'd be into getting it up the ass too, right?"

"God man, is that what I said? Did I say that? Huh, I don't know. Yeah, gotta admit, fucking Stan was fun, watching you fuck the hell out of him is fun, and the way he is taking it all, and as happy as he is, in getting it in the butt like that, there must be something to it or guys wouldn't be doing it, right? I mean, there are a lot of gay guys out there doing it, right Stan? You fuck your football boys or do they fuck you?"

"Both, but my God man, none of 'em can fuck me like you two guys can! Damn I'm so fucking glad I skipped that class I was supposed to be at this morning! Damn, this is making my week for me! Slam me man! Slam me! Come on Darrell, shoot off in my ass! Let me get it from you too! Come on man, make my ass drip with cum juices! When I leave here, I wanna be carrying some of both of you guys up in my butt!"

"Hey Stan. You said you skipped a class you were supposed to be at this morning! You here for the relationship training too?"

"Yeah, yeah, I am! I heard you two talking about the instructor that was talking about being more open with others, I figured then, that's what you guys were doing here. No, that's not why I approached you and suggested we have sex. I was just plain horny and I liked what I saw when I saw you out there on the beach. You guys here by yourselves, or are there more with you?"

"Oh no, we're not here my ourselves. There's four more of us. One more guy stays here, and the other three use the cabin next door!"

"Oh man, pound me, yeah pound my ass! We'll talk some more after I get fucked. Too hard to try and carry on a conversation when your body is jumping around, but I sure as hell am not gonna tell him to stop! Yeah, do me! Fuck me! Slam me! Let me have you! Fuck my ass! Fuck it hard!"

"I'm fucking you as hard as I can man! Damn man, how hard can you take it? You bout ready? I'm getting really, pretty close, to cumin man! I'm getting close! My dick can't hardly take too much more of this! It's so fucking hard it hurts! Here I come man – here I come! I'm cumin! I'm cummmin!"

Darrell pushed everything he had into Stan and Stan's ass, and he grabbed a hold of Stan's head with both arms and squeezed it as if he was gonna fall off of Stan's ass when he finally let the dam break loose!

"Oh yeah man! Do it! Do it! I wanna feel it hit me up in there! God man your dick is so far up in me, I hope I can feel it! Yeah, push, push, push!"

"Oh shit man, oh shit! Oh God man – I'm cummmin – I'm cummmin! Oh God, oh God man – this feels so fucking good! Oh man your ass is really grabbing my dick! Squeeze my dick! Squeeze my dick! Oh man – oh shit – what a fucking feeling! Oh Stan, I feel like I blew the hell out of your insides. You feel that?"

"Oh shit yes I felt that! It felt so damn good! Yeah, keep pushing on me, keep pushing! Keep fucking me, keep fucking me!"

Looking at Darrell, Jay asked, "Well man, what'd you think? Different, right? What do you think about fucking some guy's ass?"

Still attempting to catch his breath and talk at the same time, Darrell looked over toward Jay and replied, "Well let me put it this way man! Good! Good enough that if you plan on following through on your earlier statement about, 'missing out on something,' I'm game! I'll help you fill that void! You're the one that got me started in this, and you're the one that's gonna be back home around Philly with me, so now all I can say is, I hope like hell you can take my dick like this guy can! Jay, seriously man, this must have been something that I've been wanting to do for a long time and just never knew it! I feel like I'm a new man today, and I feel like I'm a man that knows what he is gonna need, real often! Hope you and your ass can take it! You're the only guy besides Stan here, than knows I've fucked a guy's ass, and how I'm gonna want it again, and often! So Jay, you're gonna be my man! It's gonna be me and you, doing the man fucks man thing! I think I just found what I've been missing in life! Jay, you better tell me you and your ass are gonna be ready! I mean it man! I hope you are wanting to get fucked! I mean, yeah, even yet tonight! I'm already looking forward to it!"

As Jay was starting to say something to him, Darrell continued, "Damn man! I had a couple of coaches in my past that I sure would have loved to either fuck or get fucked by if this is what it's like! Damn it – shit! Now I wonder if they were fucking around with any of my buddies and I never knew it! Boy, if I ever find out they were, I'm gonna be pissed! Not at my buddies – but at the coaches that left me out! Boy, back then, I never thought about something like that happening, but now I wonder! I do know some of 'em sure were in the coach's office a lot! Damn, now I wonder! Crap, even some of those other guys would have been fun to poke, if that's what they were doing! Shit, now I wonder just how many of the players were doing each other! Shit man, I just never imagined a coach and some football boys doing something like this together! Man, if they were and I never knew about it, I'm gonna be pissed!"

"Darrell, listen! I've never been fucked before! Darrell, I don't know if I can even take that damn big thing of yours, up in my ass or not! Darrell, I think you need some guy that gets fucked a lot! You need a man like Stan here that can take that much!"

Darrell turned, looked at Jay and said, "Jay, you'll learn to! He'll learn – won't he Stan?"

Chapter Two:
Just Go Slow!

"Hey Jay, look, I'm counting on you! Seriously man, I'm gonna need you. You're the only guy that knows that I've ever fucked some other guy, so you're the only one I can talk to about this. I can't go around telling other guys that I wanna fuck 'em. Jay, you've gotta be my man!"

"OK, tell you what! All you've done so far is to fuck Stan here, so how bout if we have Stan kind of stand by and watch while we fuck each other to just make sure we're doing stuff right? Let's face it Darrell, I'm not gonna have you fucking me with that damn big pole you've got there, without knowing that you've been fucked too. It just ain't gonna work that way. Fact is, right now I think I'd rather have Stan fuck me first, just so I kind of know what to expect before you stick all of that up in me. Seriously man – I look at that dick of yours – I think about it going up in my ass, and I shutter!"

Jay, Stan, and Darrell were just finishing up their little session of Jay and Darrell fucking the hell out of Stan's ass. Jay was, of course, not in any way acting too happy about the idea of him being the man on the bottom. On the bottom of Darrell, with that dick of his, so that Darrell will have an ass available to fuck when they get back home in Philly.

"Hey guys," Stan entered. "Why don't we do that! I mean, I'll fuck you Jay, since you think that will give you a little more confidence that, you'll then be able to take all of Darrell's rod, and if you guys want, I'll fuck Darrell so that he's been the bottom boy at least once, or Jay, if you wanna fuck him, I'll just kind of stand back and kind of coach! I'll kind of play like you are two of my football boys – I'm helping them discover the good parts of each other, and how to help the other guy feel some really good things. And you know what guys? I've actually had that happen! I've discovered that after two guys do it to each other a couple of times, they actually play together better, out on the field. For some reason, the guys that have played together, sexually, they just play together better when they're out on the field! Course, I've never been able to tell anybody just why they're working together so much better, but hey, that same thing could happen with you two! Think bout it! If you guys start fucking each other, that might make working together back at the company, a whole lot easier, and just make working, a whole hell of a lot more fun! You'll have this unspoken thing, going on between the two of you, that nobody else knows about. Hey guys – maybe there is gonna be some real good come out of attending this Inter-Relationship Training session this week. Course, don't really expect either one of you two to go back and tell the HR department just how you got so much out of the training, but if working together with each other this way, makes things easier, so be it! OK, guys! What do you wanna do? We still got some time before one of the other guys comes back to the cabin?"

"Yeah, we've got time." Darrell answered. "The other guys said they're staying for the luncheon and then wanting to hear the discussion on, 'In Office Romances.' So they should be gone until at least three or so."

"Uh, guys! I think both of you two have taken it pretty well being involved here, I mean – Darrell, you walked in on something that you sure did not expect, and Jay, when we started, you sure did not expect him to come in on us. It seems like everything's pretty OK between you two guys. Let's face it men, you two got involved in some stuff here that is really 'off of the wall' as far as just having it happen, and not expecting any of it! Darrell, you could have been really pissed when you came back here and found Jay fucking me. You took that pretty good! What about the other guys? What if one of them found out about what's going on in here today? Think they could handle it, or would there be major problems?"

Darrell looked over at Jay, and Jay returned the puzzled look. He replied, "I don't know. What you think Darrell?"

"Well, to be honest – I think Tom," then looking at Stan he added, "he's the other one staying in this cabin. I think he would probably be the coolest about it. He's young. He's only like about twenty-four. He's single. He's – ," then looking seriously at Jay he asks, "Jay, do you think he could be gay? He never talks about dates! Jay, I never thought about that! You think he could be a gay guy? Think about it! He's real quiet about his private life, he sure shows off his build whenever he gets a chance to, and I see him talking to that – kind of weird guy that works in the cafeteria, that Brad guy a lot. Now Brad – him – I'm almost sure!"

"Hey, I never thought about it either, but you are right! He never talks about having dates or anything about girls, does he? The way he's built, you'd think he'd talk about how the girls like his body and the way he looks! You know, now that I think about it, I wonder! Well – hey! Let me tell you one thing man! If he is, I'm gonna be damn glad, and you should be too!! He's gonna have to be one of your guys to use, so you can do some fucking in his ass, and not have to use my ass all the time! Shit man, now that I come to think about it, I hope like hell he is!"

Looking at Jay, Darrell asked, "How we gonna find out? How we gonna know? I can't just walk up to him and ask if he's gay or not! I can't just walk up to him, grab his crotch and then wait to see what he says!"

Looking over at Stan, Jay asked, "Hey man, willing to help us out here some?"

"Yeah, sure – yeah – I guess – how? What you talking about Jay?"

"You sure as hell managed to uncover some actions in me that I never even knew where there! I'm sure you'll have a much easier time, if it just so happens that Tom, is gay, right? He's gonna be at the cocktail hour gab-fest over in the lounge later this afternoon. How about you just kind of "meet him" and see if you can make some points with him. You'll know what to say and how to say it. See if maybe you can get him to go someplace with you, OK? He's a muscle boy, and you're a muscle boy – you should be a turn on to him if he's game and willing!"

"Yeah it's Ok, but how will I know him?"

"Oh, you'll know him! He's a good looking black man, shaved head, he'll definitely have on a tight tank top. He's got muscles and he does like for 'em to show 'em off! He's twenty-four, about five foot ten, about a hundred and ninety or a hundred and ninety-five or maybe two hundred pounds of "prime A" beef steak muscles, and no ring on the ole ring finger."

"Oh shit man, I've already met him! I met him Monday night in the cocktail lounge. He is one fucking hot man, fucking hot! He's the other one staying here!? We talked just for a few minutes. He was watching for somebody, and when that guy came in he left! He left with some other black guy! Any of your other guys with you, a black man too?"

With Jay and Darrell both breaking out into major grins, they both emphatically replied, "No! No – they're definitely not black! He left with someone else?"

"Oh, this is getting good! Got to admit I wondered that night if there could have been a possibility since they left together, right away! Men, I think we've got Tom all figured out, but we're gonna make sure later this afternoon. I'm gonna be at the gab-fest, and it's gonna be easy to strike up another conversation since we've already talked. Hey, I'll probably just ask him about the good looking guy he left with that night and see what he says! We'll do it man, we'll find out! Hey, if things go right, we could end up with a good four way here, later tonight!"

"Or maybe a five way if he and that other guy already have plans." Jay added.

"You know what Jay? I wondered just where Tom was at Monday night, but I figured it wasn't any of my business to snoop into his business. You know it was probably 12:30 or quarter till one when he came in that night. Now I bet I know! He was over at that other guy's place, doing his thing! Hey – ever looked at the ass on that guy? Tom's got a good looking bubble butt back there! Somebody could have some major fun in that ass!"

Looking squarely at Darrell, Jay asked, "So please explain to me, just how long have you been looking at other guy's bubble butts? Darrell, I thought this stuff today was supposed to be all new to you! I'm beginning to think maybe it's not all, so new, is it?"

"No – it is all new! Don't you ever look at how some other guy's built? Come on man, all guys look at other guys' butts – don't they? I mean, yeah they do – don't they? Come on here guys! Tell me, all guys look at other guys' butts, don't they?"

"Hey Darrell, I'm quite sure Stan here does – and he does a hell of a lot more with them than just look at 'em, but seriously man, I just never have! I'm sure a lot of guys never check out the ass-end on some other guy. Maybe, just maybe, you've been a little closer to wanting to do this than you realized! You've never played with some other guy before – right? Or wrong?"

"No, I've never played with some guy. Once when I was in high school, me and this other guy kinda talked about it once when we were waiting on a bus, but then we never did anything. Guess then it was just talk, just trying to be big guys. We never did anything."

"Let me tell you one thing man!" Jay interjected. "You certainly do remember that kid and your talk, don't you? I really think what I hear you saying is – you wanted to do some more stuff back then! I kind of have a feeling that if that guy, or another guy would have done something, you probably would have done something with him! Right?"

"Yeah, I think now, today anyway – I think you might be right! JJ was a little scrawny guy, but I really don't think it was because of JJ being so tinny and me being so much bigger than he was made any difference. It was the way he made me feel when we were talking about it and kinda talking about what we could do to each other. I know he must have had a little dick, well compared to me back then, but I don't think that made any difference."

"No, it sure didn't. I kind of think you like big, or you like 'em small! All I gotta says is, don't know if I'm 'the big', or I'm 'the small', but I do know my asshole is small, and when you put that damn Washington Monument up in me, you better go slow! Understand!"

"OK guys. What we gonna do? Jay, what you wanna do?"

"I wanna fuck Darrell, and if it's possible maybe while I'm fucking him, maybe you can fuck me? Can we do that? If I'm on top of him, can you get on me, 'n fuck me?"

"Yeah, yeah we can do that! We'll do ourselves a three stacker! You'll be the middle man!"

"OK guys – if I'm gonna be the social director here, Darrell lay down on your gut and Jay, spread some of this KY lube up in his ass, and some on your dick."

Spreading some of Stan's KY lube up in Darrell's ass, Jay got a big smile on his face and said, "Wow, this is fun! Shit man, I've never played with some guy's ass before, and I've got to admit, I like it! You doing OK Darrell? You've got a great ass to be feeling! God man, I never realized that fingering some other guy's ass could be so much fun! Man, this is great! Oh shit man, this is fun! Darrell, you doing OK?"

"Yeah man, yeah! I'm doing great! Push with that finger – yeah push hard! Oh shit man, I've never felt anything like that before! Shit man, I wish I could have had this done to me a long time ago! Hey Jay, put another finger up in there. Make my ass feel it! Oh yeah man, oh yeah! That's it, that's it! Oh shit man, keep it up – yeah man, keep it up! Oh Jay, go deeper, go deeper! Oh shit man now I know why guys do this! Crap man! If my coach was doing this to my buddies and I was left out, I'm gonna be pissed!

Damn, Stan, I thought fucking your ass was good, but shit man, just having some fingers moving around up in my ass is great! Come on Jay, fuck me with your dick! I wanna see what a dick feels like up in there! Oh God man! I can't believe I'm begging some guy to fuck my ass! Shit man! I never thought I'd ever be doing that! Oh shit man! I always thought I was way too macho to do anything like that! But oh I need it, oh yeah I need it! Fuck me man, fuck me!"

"OK Jay, get ready to put it up in him, he's ready! He's real ready! Just go slow. Every asshole needs to open up some when getting something put up in there, so just go in slow, but once you're up in there, then he'll start begging for more! Yeah, that's right, that's good! How you doing Darrell, feeling OK?"

"Oh shit yes, I'm doing great! Oh man, I thought getting fucked in your ass was supposed to be something bad! Fuck man, this is great! Yeah Jay, push it in! Yeah push it in! I can tell you're in me, push it all the way in! Yeah, I can feel it, yeah it's feeling great! Yeah man, fuck me, fuck me!"

Jay laid the rest of the way down on top of Darrell and made a bed out of him, as he listened to Darrell beg for more dick. He heard the begging, and he then gave him all he had.

"Oh God man, I've got it don't I? I've got all of your dick don't I? Jay, I've got all of your dick, don't I?"

"Yeah man, yeah, you've got it! Like it? How's it feeling?"

"Oh man, it's feeling good, damn good! Jay, how big is your dick? How much is up in me?"

"Hell man, I don't know! I've never measured it! How do I know?"

"Hey Darrell, I think his dick is just about seven and a half or eight inches long, and it's thick! I always know what I'm about to get fucked with when I'm about to get it in the ass, and that's what I'd guess from my looking at it, before he poked me. I think his and mine are about the same length, but his is a lot thicker than mine. He's got a thick dick! It's gonna open your asshole! You've feel it! Well, from what you're saying, I guess maybe you are feeling it, aren't you?"

"Oh shit man! If his is like seven and a half or eight and it feels this fucking good up in there, I wonder what in the hell my nine of ten incher must feel like? Oh shit man, I love this! Jay, fuck me, let me feel you up in there! Pound me please! Yeah, I want to know what it can feel like getting rammed and slammed! Do it man, do it!"

Jay did! He knew his co-worker was now in the need, and he was gonna do everything he could, to make sure that he made that man know, he had been fucked, and fucked good! This was Jay's first time in some guy's ass, and the way Darrell was begging for it, Jay wanted to deliver. He decided that if he was gonna be the taker of that enormous rod of Darrell's, then he'd better make sure Darrell enjoyed getting it up in the ass too, since it was sounding like there were gonna be plenty of play sessions coming up in the near future!

"Like it? You like it Darrell? Do I feel good? Like it?"

"Oh God yes Jay, God yes! Oh shit man, I am so fucking glad I came back here when I did! Oh shit man I wish I'd been doing this years ago! Damn man, what a way to go! Oh I love this! I'll never make some bad, nasty, fucking comment about a gay again! Crap man, they're the ones that know how in the hell to fucking live! Oh God, can you imagine two guys living together and getting to do this every night? Oh man, why didn't I get fucked when I was in school? Oh fuck man, I wish the coach would have fucked me back then! Oh man, I love this – fuck me – fuck me! Fuck me harder – yeah harder man, harder! Slam my ass!"

Stan was rather sitting back watching Jay and Darrell go at it. He had intended to get up on Jay's butt and fuck him while Jay was in Darrell, but after the session got going, he decided that trying to do a three stack while Jay was pumping that much, and that wildly, just was not gonna work. He had not expected Darrell to want fucked so wildly or forcefully, and he was quite pleased that Jay was performing up to standard, since Darrell's butt was the first one he had ever been in before!

"Darrell, Darrell, I'm gonna cum! Hang on man, I'm gonna cum!!!!!! I gotta cum – I gotta cum! Oh man – here it comes – here it comes!!!!!! Oh shit man – oh shit! Oh damn man! My dick was pinched so fucking tight up in there – trying to let my juice out was trouble. Man, I just knew I had to let it go, but man, my dick was slammed shut so tight I couldn't cum! Oh wow! Oh shit man, Darrell, you OK? You feel that!?"

"Oh fucking shit man, hell yes I felt that! Damn man, how much load did you give me? Damn I feel like when I stand up, my ass is gonna flow! Wow! Oh shit, so that's what it feels like to get shot up in the ass! Oh God man, great, just plain great! Thanks man, thanks Jay!"

"Don't need to thank me man – I liked that! You've got one fucking hot ass to play with man! Solid as hell and it feels good! Your asshole is so fucking tight, God it feels good! Damn, now I'm looking forward to being back in Philly! Shit man, I'm gonna need that all the time too! If you're gonna fuck me, then I'm gonna be fucking you too!"

Then laying there and recuperating on Darrell, Jay turned his head and asked, "Hey, I thought you were gonna do me while I did him? What happened? You never got up on, or in me!"

"Yeah, I know! Seriously man, I did not expect Darrell to go so wild! The way you were humping and fucking him, there was no way in hell I could ever start to aim my dick at your asshole – let alone get it in. I decided I'd just wait till you exploded off in him, and you two got done. Now that you've fucked him, and he's been fucked, I think what we need to do next is let him get his dick up in you! I don't think after that little session you're gonna need me to do you first. I think it's time you find out for yourself, just how great his dick is gonna feel going up inside of you! I know right now you've got some scares and some apprehensions about being able to take him, but man, believe me, once you've got it up in you, you are gonna go crazy for it! You saw how crazy he went, wanting you and your dick and how fucking wild he was for it! And that was the first time he'd ever been fucked! Well, now I think you need to see for yourself, just how great your ass can feel with him up inside of you! You 'bout ready to get fucked, and get fucked, big time? You ain't never had it before, and today's your day, and you're gonna start out with, 'the dick of death'! He's hungry for you and I know damn well you're hungry for it! I'll be here and make sure everything goes OK – OK? Ready?"

"Yeah come on Jay, come on! I wanna know I can fuck you! Come on man, let me at you! I wanna fuck you!"

Chapter Three:
Out of This World Man!

"OK Jay, everything's gonna be OK. I know the first time is a little intimidating, and especially when it's gonna be with a dick like Darrell's but you gotta trust me man, once you've had it, you're gonna be begging for it all the time. Come on Darrell, get a good coating of KY on that thing and Jay, just lay down there and relax. He ain't gonna hurt you any!"

Stan was of course acting like the coach, and he definitely had his hands full in getting Jay to realize that getting Darrell's oversized rod pushed up in his ass was gonna be a good and an exciting thing, not some action of major pain. Jay laid down on the bed, ass up in the air, and Darrell, with his dick now well coated with KY, slid up on top of him, and aimed his dick at Jay's butt hole.

"Now just go slow Darrell." Stan instructed and encouraged. "Jay's totally convinced that when you push that up in him, he's gonna totally fall apart, in ripped and torn pieces, so go slow so he can take it and enjoy it like it's intended for."

Darrell positioned himself so that he had good position in control, and did not unintentionally lean down onto Jay too much. He knew he needed to start this fuck with about as much care and patience as he could. He knew he sure could not go up and into Jay with the same gusto that he had when he fucked Stan. Stan was experienced and hungry for it, where Jay had never been fucked before, and he sure was not too convinced that everything was gonna go OK.

Ever so slowly Darrell started to lower himself down onto Jay's ass and let his cock start its slow entry into Jay's nervous as hell asshole.

Jay tried to keep himself calm and just lay there without expressing any anxiety or fear for what was about to happen, but keeping himself under calm control was a major problem. He tried to look back at Darrell and say, "Darrell, please, please go slow! Please if it hurts too much, you'll stop, right? Please man, please promise me you'll stop if I tell you to, OK?"

"OK, OK! Calm down man, just calm down! I'm going real slow, and I'm listening to you. Just let your ass relax. Let your butt just lay there and don't try pinching it shut. I'll go slow! Seriously man, I'll go slow. I want you to enjoy this! I really do!"

"Oh, ouch! Oh shit man, shit! Damn man, oh crap that hurt! God Darrell, that did hurt there for a second."

"Hey the head of my dick just popped in. Sorry bout that, but it had to punch your little hole open enough to slide up in there. It's in now. Feeling OK?"

"Yeah I am now, but shit man it hurt there for a second or two. Damn don't do that again!"

"Oh no, I won't. We just had to get your little trap door back there to snap open so I could get in there. I'm in now. That won't happen again!"

As Darrell was talking to Jay, he was continuing his ever so slight entry into Jay's ass, and was successfully opening Jay's ass ever so slowly that his dick was actually sliding in, and Jay did not quite realize it. Slowly, and with a lot of hand movements along Jay's body, up along his neck, down along the sides of his hips and down along his legs, Darrell was keeping Jay's attention away from his ass, and at the same time making great strides in going up and into the warm chute!

Jay was quite unconscious about just how much dick he had been taking, although he had started expressing some sounds of comfort when he would slightly utter, "Yeah, yeah! Yeah, how you doing? You going in any?"

As Darrell rubbed Jay's shoulders and the back of his neck, he replied, "Yeah some. Just some. Just lay there, we're in no hurry! We'll just take this good and slow." Then turning to look at Stan, Darrell let out a major grin, as he and Stan shared the secret that Darrell was now almost all the way up and in Jay.

"Hey Jay, my man, how you doing?" Darrell asked as he laid full length on Jay's back.

"I'm OK right now. I'm just trying to lay here and relax and wait for you to finish putting some more of that thing up in me. How much you got in me? You've just got a little in me, right? Like what, about maybe two or three inches?"

"Yeah Jay, yeah! Yeah I've got two or three inches up in you, plus about eight more. Jay – you have my whole dick up in you! You've got the whole damn thing man, the whole thing!"

Then as Darrell finished that statement, he pushed strongly with his torso onto Jay's body so that Jay could tell from his position that Darrell did, in-fact, have all of his dick up in him, since he pushed up against his body with full force, and their bodies were in total contact.

"Oh shit man, you kidding? Darrell, you don't have that whole thing up in me already – do you?"

"Yes – oh yes I do man, the whole thing! See, it's pretty good ain't it? Feeling pretty good? How you feeling? Feeling OK?"

"Oh shit man, you can't have! Seriously man, you don't have all of that up in me do you? Come on Darrell, tell me the truth. You can't have all of that thing up in me yet, do you?"

"Yeah, I do! Yes Jay, yeah, you've got the whole thing! You took it all! You didn't know it was going up in there like that did you?"

"No hell no! Hell man, you sure? Stan, he got all of it up in me? Come on guys, don't lie to me! How much dick he got up in me Stan?"

"Jay, you've got his whole stick up in you! You've got it all man, you've got it all! Not so bad now is it? Feeling pretty good?"

"Oh shit man, I can't believe this! Seriously guys, I have that whole fucking thing up in me? Are you kidding?"

"No Jay, we're not kidding. I've got the whole thing up in you. Want me to pull it back some so you can feel it moving up in there?"

"Yeah, yeah! Yeah Darrell, yeah let me feel it."

Jay laid there completely shocked that he had, unknowingly, taken all of Darrell's enormous dick up into his ass, and he was now asking for Darrell to move it around some so he could feel it up in himself.

"Oh shit man, oh shit! Yeah, do that, do that! Oh Darrell, wow! Oh shit! Oh God man, that feels good! Yeah, keep that up. Yeah, pull out a little farther, yeah, yeah man, I like that! OK man, push it back in me! Yeah, push on me hard! Real hard! Oh man, how in the hell could I think that was gonna hurt? Oh shit man, fuck me, fuck me!"

Sitting on the edge of the bed, beside the two now fucking co-workers, Stan reached over placed his hand on Jay's head and asked, "Like it? Feels pretty good don't it? Like having Darrell up inside of you? Like him fucking you and that cute little ass of yours? Like it?"

Turning his head so he could see Stan, Jay answered. "Oh shit man, I can't believe this! Seriously man, I thought it was gonna hurt like hell to have him and that damn dick of his up inside of me! Stan, this feels good! Oh man, it's good! It only hurt for that one or two seconds when his dick head went in and pushed my asshole open, and after that I thought he was just laying there and not pushing any. Seriously man, I did not know he was putting that thing up in me! I thought I just had the tip of it in me. Oh Darrell, fuck me! Push it in all the way. Let me feel it up in there man, let me feel it! Oh shit man, this is great! Yeah guys, I like this! Oh crap! Why in the hell was I so fucking afraid of this? Oh man, this is great! I love this! Yeah Darrell, fuck me, let me feel it man, let me feel it!"

"Fuck him Darrell, fuck him. He's wanting it now, he's wanting to feel that dick of yours up in him. Yeah man, yeah, that's the way. Pound his ass. He's into this now! He's got one hell of a big grin on his face, he likes what's happening back there! Do him!"

For about ten minutes or more, Darrell enjoyed the initial entrance into the virgin ass, and likewise Jay not only enjoyed it, but kept begging for, "More, harder, yeah man, more! Yeah you can fuck me anytime you want now man! Hell man, I'm anxious to get back to Philly and be your bottom guy now! Oh shit man, I cannot believe having something that big, that stiff, and having it going in and out of you like it is, can feel so fucking good! Oh shit man, why in the hell wasn't I getting fucked earlier. Man alive, am I fucking glad the company sent us on this little learning session this week! I think I've already learned a hell of a lot more than what we were expected to learn, and hell man, we've got three more days here to keep learning stuff. Shit man, if it's all this good, I could stay here and learn for another week or two."

"Hey guys," Stan entered, "I'm feeling kind of out of the action here. Let's do something that I think both of you guys will like. Jay, stand up here and lean up against this door frame. Stand there and lean forward with your arms and hands up about here. Yeah! Darrell, come up behind him and fuck his ass! Yeah, do a stand up fuck! I think you'll like it!"

Jay got into position, and Darrell moved up behind him, and pushed it in!

"Oh shit man, oh shit! Oh God I like that! Oh Darrell, push man, push! Oh shit, this does feel good! Yeah Stan, I like this!"

As Jay was now getting it up the ass, in a standing position, and he was discovering how getting fucked while standing up can be as much fun a laying down, Stan positioned himself down in front of Jay, and moved in on his dick.

"Oh shit man, you gonna suck on me? Stan, you gonna suck on my dick?"

Looking up toward Jay, Stan replied, "Yeah, that OK? Can I suck you?"

"Oh shit yeah, but oh man, I never thought about you doing that! Oh Stan, I've never been sucked on before! Oh shit man that is making my dick hard – oh man – oh fuck! Oh fuck! Oh fuck man – that is great! Oh God Darrell, he's sucking on my dick! Oh God man, he's got my dick down his throat!"

"Yeah I see it, I see it! Oh man, I sure did not expect that! Oh Jay, how's that feeling? How's that feeling on your dick?"

"Oh shit man, how in the hell can I say! 'Oh God man, I'm getting it up in the ass and now I'm getting my dick sucked on too! Oh shit man. Oh, God.'"

Stan pulled off just quickly enough to say, "Hey, Darrell – reach around and pinch his tits some. Pinch 'em, just kind of soft though!"

As Darrell did, Jay let out an, "Oh shit man, oh shit! Oh God man – I've never felt anything like that in my entire life! Oh shit man, pinch 'em, pinch 'em! Oh guys, I'm in heaven, I'm in fucking heaven! Oh man I can't believe this!"

With Stan's back and the back of his head up against the door frame, he was taking Jay's cock deeper and deeper each time Darrell rammed Jay's ass. He was rather trapped between the door frame and Jay's body. He didn't complain though, he liked being in the position where each time Darrell rammed forward into Jay's ass, it forced Jay's dick back into his mouth, again and again! Darrell was slamming Jay's ass, and Jay was slamming Stan's mouth. All three men were definitely happy and not complaining any.

"Oh Jay, I'm getting real close to cumin here man, I'm getting real close! You ready to take a load up your ass? I'm gonna do it man! I'm gonna to it!"

"Oh, so am I man, so am I! Stan, can I cum in your mouth? Stan, I'm gonna cum too!"

Stan uttered a muffled, "Yeah, yeah," but with his mouth full of dick, that was as much as he could manage to do.

"Oh God – oh God – oh God! Here it comes man – here it comes!" Darrell let out with the squeals of, "Oh God," as he pushed his rod up and into Jay's ass, just as far as he could manage – right as his load flew out!

"Oh shit man, me too!" Jay almost shouted. "Oh Stan, get ready man, get ready! I'm cumin man – I'm cummmmin! Oh shit man, I'm in fucking heaven man, I'm in heaven! Oh shit! There is no way a guy can have a better cum shot than that! A dick of death up in my ass pushing in me as far as possible, a man sucking on my dick and sucking all the cum out of it, feeling like a big Hoover vacuum cleaner working on it, and then getting both of my tits pinched – oh my God man – nothing else could have been done to me to make that anymore exciting! Oh shit man, wow! Out of this world man! Out of this world!"

"Oh shit man, how's your ass Jay? God oh mighty, I slammed the hell out of that thing! Shit man, I love fucking your ass! God is it tight and sweet! Wow, what a fuck! Oh man, now you really gotta promise me that when we get back to Philly, you gotta promise me you'll let me do you, and your ass and do you often. Oh man, what a fucking trip! Hey, how're your tits? I never thought about playing with 'em until Stan told me to get 'em. Did that feel good? Like that?"

"Oh man, hell yeah! Pinching and playing with my tits was something I never thought of, but man – anytime you're fucking my ass, you reach around and fuck with my tits! Yeah, that was great! Hey Stan, thanks for telling him to do that! God that felt good! God man, what a fucking experience! Hey Stan, how you doing?"

"Hey, I'm doing great, just great! You got sweet cum man, real sweet cum! You kind of taste like some of my football boys do. I always thought theirs tasted sweet since they are so young, but man alive, I just found me a guy that's not a college kid anymore, and he's got sweet cum too! Darrell, you might want to taste that sometime."

"Oh, shit, I don't know! Suck on his dick? I don't know! Jay, would you do that, I mean suck on some guy's dick? Oh man, I never thought about doing that to some guy!"

"Hey man, this morning at ten, I would have sworn I'd never be fucking some guy's ass nor letting some guy put his dick up in my ass, but –what – about three hours later, I've now fucked a coach – a guy I didn't even know until about ten o'clock, I've fucked a co-worker, that I sure as hell did not know swung a baseball bat for a dick, and I've also been fucked by that bat – so don't ask me now what I will or will not do. All of a sudden, I'm finding out I am a little more willing to do things that I never thought I'd ever do, so don't ask. Gotta admit, even when we started this earlier today, the idea of sucking or getting sucked on never occurred to me, that is until Stan got down there and put my dick in his mouth. That's when all of a sudden I realized that sucking, or getting sucked, is probably part of this man-on-man playing around, so yeah, it's made me wonder just what I will do next. I'll never say never, I just don't know anymore! I will say one thing though – anytime some guy wants to take it out and suck on it, it's all his! Especially if he can suck on it as hard as Stan does. I thought for a few minutes there, you were gonna actually suck the tip off of it! Man it felt like it was about to fall off! Stan, I have to assume you've sucked on a lot of college football dicks? What all you do with those guys? You usually just do the football boys, or you have other guys to use too?"

"Oh, I've got more than just the football guys – but I've got to admit, they're usually the most fun. They're horny and anxious! They've all got good stiff dicks and they're ready whenever possible."

"Like what you mean, whenever? Ever done any of 'em, in some rather funny situations? Are you the one that always approaches 'em, or do they let you know when they want something?"

"Oh yeah, they definitely let me know! Probably the weirdest time was one night after a sports banquet at the student lounge. I was the Master of Ceremony for the program, and so I was one of the last ones to leave after the banquet. I went out to the parking lot to leave, and had two guys sitting out there waiting on me."

"Two, two at the same time?" Jay quickly asked?

"Yeah, two! Guy by the nickname of Bucky – he was one of my football boys, and a guy by the name of Jerry. Jerry was Bucky's cousin – in town just to attend the banquet, since Bucky was given an outstanding player award. Two of the hottest bodies I have ever played with! See Bucky and I had been doing it for – oh, probably maybe almost a year, but the Jerry guy, I didn't even know him! When I got over close to where they were, Bucky introduced me to Jerry, and told me who he was. Told me he had told Jerry that we play around together and he begged Bucky to get him involved. They told me he had played with some of his friends back home, some, but he really wanted to be involved in a three way, so they wanted to know if I'd play. Bucky told me that he didn't think I'd mind if they asked, since he was pretty sure I probably wanted to go play anyway. He knew it had been a week or more since I'd had one of the guys, and he knew I would be real ready at the first chance I got. Well, that was the first chance, and yes, I took it! Jerry was staying at a motel in town, so we made use of it!"

"Hey, that Bucky and his cousin, Jerry – had they ever played together before? Had they fucked around with each other before?" Darrell asked with sincere interest.

"No, guess not! They told me that Bucky found out about Jerry's playing around earlier that afternoon when Bucky thought he was gonna shock the hell out of Jerry by laughing and trying to make a joking statement about how he always thought I was kind of hot, 'If you like guys, that is,' he had said, and how he wondered just what he'd do if I kind of came onto him sometime. He told me that he had told Jerry, that he had heard about coaches and some players that do the sex thing together. That made Jerry ask him if he'd ever played with another guy before, and that really opened up the conversation. Both of them finally admitted that they each do play around, and Bucky finally admitted that he and I were doing it about every other week or so. I guess that's when Jerry told him he really wanted to do a three way, if Bucky had the nerve to ask me to do it! Well, Bucky told me later he had to do it, or he was afraid Jerry would think he was just shitting him. So anyway, I got to play with two of the hottest built guys that I ever had at the same time. Bucky was built like a brick shit house, but his cousin Jerry – now there was a body that finally ended up on the cover of some workout mags! You know, the big muscle boys that are always holding about seventy-five pounds of dumbbells in their hands. Well, about three or four years later, I actually saw him on a cover. Bucky was long gone by that time, so I never got to talk to Bucky about it, but it sure gave me a new ragging, big, hard on when I saw that cover. Just the idea that I had fucked that guy and been fucked by him, was an all new turn-on! I think I abused that body rougher that night than any other body I ever played with. And how he loved it! Bucky was amazed at how much rough and tumble stuff he wanted and begged for! He actually begged for me and Bucky to get real rough with him, all at the same time. He really was into some deep S&M, but we didn't have any equipment to use, so we just had to use our hands and slap the hell out of his ass, as much as we could. Bucky told me later he sure as hell did not know his cousin played with guys until that conversation earlier that day, and he sure didn't know he was really into the S&M, stuff until after we got to playing around. That Jerry had the body of death and a dick to go with it. Big, but still not as big as yours Darrell!"

"Shit man! For somebody that's never even played with some guy until today, listening to that sure has made me feel all turned on!" Darrell stated. "God man, listening to that is so fucking hot! You suppose that's kind of the way I am, but I just don't know it?"

"Could be!" Stan answered. "You know what I'm real interested in right now is – how your buddy Tom is hung? He's one hot looking black man, and all my hot looking, black football boys always have a sausage hanging on 'em that all the other guys peek a look at whenever they think they can get away with it! I always get such a kick out of it when some guy really wants to see some other guy's big dick, and in his nervous attempt to catch a glimpse of it, he kind of fails to realize maybe somebody else is watching him – somebody like me. Hey guys, that's how I find my next and new playmate! Watch and see which ones like to check out the big swingers!"

"Stan, how do you let them know you're game? What do you do to find out if they're players? I just can't imagine getting to find out if some football player is game or not. What do you do?"

"Hey Jay, all you gotta do is watch. Like I just said about 'em watching some other guy's dick swinging in the breeze. Whenever I happen to see one of 'em checking out some other guy, I just casually happen to mention it to him as soon as possible. If I see, let's say Jimmy checking out Sammy and his wammy, whenever I get a chance to talk to Jimmy, I usually just say something like, 'Hey, saw you checking out Sammy's equipment. Pretty damn big piece of meat, ain't' it?" They're usually pretty shocked that I mentioned it, but at the same time, they're kind of anxious to talk about it, and a little more than eager to make some positive comments about what it looked like. Hey, from there, it's the casual conversation about how much fun it'd be, to maybe pull on it, to see what he'd do, and step by step work up to where and when I'm comfortable that he's kind of into it. Then I admit I've jerked on some dicks before, and I just wonder if jerking on Sammy's would be like some of the ones I've jerked on before. Believe it or not, when they hear that, almost every fucking time, they start rubbing their own crotch without realizing it. I let them know I'm watching, they know I'm watching 'em playing with themselves, and from that time on, it's yeah – he wants it, yeah – he admits it, and yeah – I let him know I'll help him out if he wants to feel something really good! Hey, just asking the question, the big question is enough to make almost any of 'em immediately drop their drawers and pull it out."

"The question – the big question? What's the question?" Jay asked as Darrell chipped in a, "Yeah, what's the question?"

"It's just the, 'Hey guy, wanna play with the coach some? Wanna feel the coach's? Coach'll play with someone that looks like you!' Then I tell 'em, I wanna see how their big dick feels. Doesn't need to be a big dick, but ya tell all of 'em the same thing! They all wanna think they've got a big dick! And just the idea that their coach wants to play with it, really gets them all hot and bothered!"

"Uh, Stan, have all of these guys played around before, or not? Like do they know what's going on?" Jay inquired with an increased sense to interest.

"You know guys. I've been playing around with college guys for like six years now, and I've only had one guy that I know was a total virgin. Hey, let's face it, they are all sports jocks, and they have girls and guys all over them all the time, so they get started in the ole sex scene pretty early. The ones I usually end up playing with are the ones that have already decided they'd rather date the Homecoming King, rather than the Homecoming Queen. They've already decided which side of the field they're gonna play on. That's why the big swinging dicks in the shower room are so interesting to them."

"Stan, you ever have one guy tell you that some other guy wants to do it too? Like one friend telling you about some guy you had never done before?"

"Oh yeah! Yeah that actually happens a lot more often than you'd expect. Two guys that used to play together, and then maybe one graduates or transfers to another school, then they tell me about the guy they are leaving behind. They don't feel like they've walked out on their buddy, that way! Yeah – I've had, and gained, some pretty damn good sex that way! Hey, the guy that was leaving, liked him and the way he played, so he wanted to make sure he was all set up, after he was gone. And yeah, I've had the guys that wanted to do a three way, so they tell me about one of the other guys that I've never fucked with before."

"After you got out of college, you sure didn't start at the university level right away did you? Did you coach in a high school first?"

"Oh yeah! Yeah I did – for five years! And no – I did not play with the high school guys! Too young! But, I got lucky at the end of my first year!"

"What you mean you got lucky? How? What happened? Jay and Darrell both asked.

"It was during spring break and I was in St. Louis. The high school was about twenty-five or thirty miles outside of St. Louis. Anyway, I was in a gay bar one night, and low 'n behold, one of my football player's Dad came in. Of course he was shocked and pretty scared to see me there, and he really didn't know how to handle it, but I quickly put him at ease. I told him he sure as hell, was of a lot more exciting to me than some high school kids were, and of course I sure wasn't gonna tell anybody back home that we were in a gay bar together. He didn't have any sex buddies to play with back home – small town, so for the next four years, I took care of this Daddy, and that Daddy took care of me! I lived out on an old farm, and it was real convenient for him to just happen out there about every week or so! His boy never found out that his coach and his own daddy were fucking and sucking each other! Damn he was good too! Kept my cum bag emptied so that I didn't start looking at stuff I shouldn't be looking at. It was then, that I moved and got the job at State, and started meeting and then playing with some of the college guys. Took me a few months at first to get started, but once I kind of learned how to do the slow and easy approach, things went pretty well! I still like the senior guys the best, but damn it, they graduate and then leave town. So I've got to keep developing new guys. The shower room is definitely a plus for me. I just need to make it all look very casual, and not let anybody know why I just happen in there, right as the uniforms and the towels come off!"

"Well, I'll assume you're gonna plan on using the same calm manner to figure out if our man Tom is gay or not, right?" Darrell asked as he was gaining more and more intense interest, about if Tom was or was not a gay guy! Darrell's new sex actions this day had definitely helped his sexual interest in Tom grow, and grow largely! He had openly stated, emphatically, that he did hope like hell, that Tom was gay. He had stated that he wanted to play with that man!

"Yeah, I am. But men, I'd better be getting out of here if I'm gonna be over at the gab-fest to try and meet up with him. You guys mind if I take a quick shower and kind of freshen up some before I head over there? I need to be moving – the time is slipping by pretty fast."

"No, not a problem at all!" Jay responded. "Fact is Darrell and I kind of need to do the same thing. Let me grab you a towel from the closet."

Stan quickly lathered up and rinsed off, and Jay then started to shower. As he was showering, Darrell was slightly straightening up the cabin some, so that things did not appear to be all out of place, when Jay rather hollered out to Stan, "Hey Stan! What do you plan on doing if Tom does agree to go someplace with you? You gonna take him to your place or bring him here or what?"

Also with somewhat of a slight yell, just loud enough so that Jay could hear over the sound of the shower, Stan replied, "I'm just not sure yet! You think I oughta bring him come back here? I've gonna tell him sometime, somehow – that we've all been fucking around! When do you think should I tell him that?"

Just as Stan hollered that back to Jay, Darrell was attempting to get Stan's attention by yelling, and kind of waving his arms. "Uhhh guys, guys, guys!!"

Although Jay could not, and did not hear Darrell, Stan did. He stood up, and as he continued to wipe his ass and his dick dry, he turned to look at Darrell. His mouth flew open and under his breath he said, "Oh my god! Oh shit!"

Just as Stan straightened up and turned toward Darrell to see what he was yelling about, Jay turned off the water, came out of the shower, and after seeing Stan's shocked expression, he turned to see – whatever it was – that was shocking Stan so badly. Standing there, fully wet, and his yet partial hard on sticking straight out, he too uttered an emphatic, but much louder, "Oh my God! Oh shit!"

Chapter Four:
"*Big, Ain't A Big Enough Word For That Thing!*"

"God man – what in the hell is going on here?" Tom emphatically asked as he checked out the scene of Jay, Stan and Darrell – all standing there fully bare assed and naked!

"Tom, when in the hell did you come in? Hey man, let me explain here!" Jay rattlingly asked, and stated, almost all at the same time, "Tom, let me explain, let me explain!"

"Hey Jay, I don't think you need to explain anything, but I am real confused about you being here too Darrell!" Tom stated quite matter of factly, as he looked at Darrell.

"Wait a minute – wait a minute!" Jay quite anxiously jumped in. "Wait a minute! What'd you mean I don't need to explain anything, but you are shocked that Darrell's here too? What do you mean? What are you saying?"

"Well, I kind of knew earlier this morning that you and, Stan – Stan, right? – were obviously going to be doing stuff when I saw you two leaving the beach shower area – well – kinda with your hands all over each other."

"What? What? What!?" Jay kept asking in a total state of confusion.

"Hey! Stan and I met each other over at the lounge the other night, and I knew then he was gay! Sorry Stan, but the way you were trying to hit up on me that night, it was pretty damn obvious! So, this morning when I saw you two showering together, then leaving the area with your hands all over each other – hell, I knew it was gonna be play time. My big shock though is, that Darrell's involved. Jay, I thought I was kind of shocked when I saw you, leaving with Stan – but I sure never expected to find Darrell all involved, too!"

"Tom, how in the hell did you see us this morning? Where in the hell were you? There wasn't anybody around when we showered!"

"Hey Jay, the outdoor coffee shop is right across the street! If you just happen to be sitting, up close, by the hedge along the front, you can see the whole shower area and the beach area from there. I was there and I just happened to see you two taking a shower, then walking away – and should I say, acting like some pretty close friends?"

"Yeah but we didn't do anything there at the shower! We just showered and then left!"

"Yeah you left, but Jay – weren't you aware that Stan here, had his hand on the back of your trunks? He was grabbing your ass as you two walked away! Pretty damn obvious you two were headed for a room someplace, so I stayed away from here, figuring that this is where you'd be headed. My shock though – like I said – is that Darrell was part of it! Hey guys, why in the hell didn't you guys let me know – way before this – that you guys play around? I'm game! I've done it – well maybe you guys just aren't aware, but – hell yes, I'm gay! Shit man, how long you two been playing with each other?"

Once Tom made the statement that he was gay, the tension definitely loosened up a bit, well actually, a lot, and a lot of explaining went on about how everything had just happened that day. Everybody was still pretty confused about all the details, but much more relaxed knowing that nobody was gonna be all upset – at what was happening, and – had already happened, that day.

During the ensuing talking and explaining of details and situations, Tom did say, "Yeah that was Bobby – my main man, that came into the lounge Monday night, that I left with. He travels for his company, and we had it all arranged, that since he can schedule his own business trips, we decided that while I was here, it'd be a good time for him to schedule his trip into his South Carolina territory. Then, we could see each other a couple of times this week. I went with him to his motel room that night and we fucked for a couple of hours. That's where I was, that night. Man, too bad you two hadn't started doing the 'boy-toy' thing until today! Monday night would've been a good time for you two to have gotten it on, since I was gone until late! And, of course, if you two had known about me, then I could have just spent the rest of the night with Bobby and getting my rocks off a couple more times!"

Looking at, and smiling toward Tom, Stan stated, "Gotta tell you man, you did good for yourself! Is he your partner or just a good, solid, friend?"

"No, he's my partner. We've been together for three years now. Love the hell out of that guy!"

Looking at Jay and Darrell, Stan added. "He's got a real hottie men – a real hottie! I mean, Tom, you're a hottie too, but your man Bobby, now he is a real man! What does he do for a living? Sell barbells that he carries around with him all day? Men, he is hot guys – he is hot! Creamed my jeans over that one, the night I saw him come in and get Tom. Damn, I wanted to go too!"

"Actually he's a lumber salesman that calls on lumber stores. I always joke with him that he's always got a long, stiff, hard, woody somewhere, close by!"

"Hey man! Speaking of long stiff hard ones," Jay interjected, "I will admit we've been wondering about yours. I don't know if you ever saw this one over here before today – but we're wondering how you compare to that big "swonger" that Darrell's carrying between his legs!"

Looking over toward Darrell with a big grin on his face, Tom stated. "I don't know! When I came in, and kind of shocked the hell out of all three of you guys, Darrell – you grabbed that pair of shorts so damn fast I never really got a good look at it. I do remember one day in the men's room at the company I almost got a glimpse of it, well anyway enough that I've always wondered about it ever since then – so come on man, pull it out, let me finally see it! From the big bulge in the crotch you're showing there, I assume it's a big one, right? Is it big guys?"

"Hey man, 'big' ain't a big enough word for that thing!" Jay emphatically stated! "Come on Darrell, you just might as well let Tom see it now! The rest of us are standing here bare assed naked, and letting it all show, let him see it!"

Hearing Jay's encouragement to just take it out and let Tom see it, he finally did, but then commented, "But it's soft now. It's not so big when it's soft."

Unfastening his own pants, pulling them open, pulling his briefs down, and then pulling his own rod out, Tom said, "Hey, here's mine, grab it – let me grab yours, and we'll just get both of 'em hard, then do a little compare, OK?"

Now with Darrell and Tom – dick in hand – Stan and Jay took an identical position, and four dicks were being jerked on all at the same time.

"Oh yes man! Oh yes!" Stan emphatically stated, as he got Jay's meat good and stiff, and then knelt down in front of it and swallowed the full length.

Looking over at Stan's actions on Jay's rod, Tom stated, "Hey, that looks like the thing to do! Look at the size of this fucker here, guys! Don't know if I can take all of it or not, so give me oxygen if I pass out on it, but I'm gonna try!" And with that stated, Tom too was down on his knees and was now pushing his mouth onto Darrell's cock stick! It took a couple of deep breaths to finally get the entire length down into the back of his throat, but with his excitement and his anxiety of having a hold of this much meat, and being white meat too, just made Tom that much more determined to take the whole, stiff, thick, thing!

"Oh my God man! Oh my God!" Darrell almost shouted out in glee! "Oh man, do me, do me! Oh I've never had something like this done on my dick before! Oh Tom, suck me man, suck me!"

Tom had managed to swallow just about three fourths of Darrell's rod, and he was sucking on it as hard as he could! He knew from what he had been told, this was Darrell's first blow job, and he wanted it to be a good one! He wanted Darrell to remember this with good thoughts, and besides, once they were back in Philly, Tom knew he was gonna want this big cock stuck back in his throat more than just once!

Once again, as had just happened a short time earlier, Stan was now completely on Jay's shaft, and he was sucking everything out of it possible. He had Jay backed up against a wall so that when he forced his face forward, Jay's body was locked into position and could not move back any. Stan was taking all of it, and Jay was helping him by grabbing hold of the sides of his head and pulling him forward as much as possible.

Suddenly, the room was almost totally silent – excusing the moaning and the groaning that Darrell and Jay were so emphatically expressing – Darrell slapped Tom on the shoulder and quite emphatically said, "Tom, Tom! Tom – I gotta shoot! Hey guy, guy, I gotta shoot!"

With his head firmly positioned without any movement possible, Tom uttered a weak, "Ok, ok!" He attempted to shake his head up and down, in an attempt to tell Darrell to unload, and unload in his throat!

"Oh shit! Oh shit! Me too!" Jay firmly stated as he heard Darrell make his statement of climax! "Oh Stan, get ready – get ready – I'm just about there! Oh man – here it cummmmmms, here it cummmmmms! Oh man, oh shit! Oh man! I thought I was empty already! Oh shit man, what a feeling! Oh man, oh Stan, thanks! Thanks! Oh my dick is so fucking happy, so fucking happy! Happy, but drained! Wow man, wow!"

Stan pulled off of Jay, looked up at him, smiled, wiped his mouth and said, "Hot! Fucking hot man – you are fucking hot! Damn man, you have got good cum! Good fresh, new cum! Good tasting cum! Thanks again, thanks again! I love to suck your cock!"

Just as Stan was expounding the sweet praises of Jay's male juices, Darrell let out an unidentifiable yell, grabbed Tom's head on each side, and locked himself onto, and into, Tom's mouth as he thrust his body forward and unloaded all of his hot, sweet, thick, man cum into Tom's throat! "Oh man! Oh man! Oh Tom, oh Thomas – Thomas – Thomas! Oh man, oh shit! Oh guy – you OK? Oh – I have never shot off in someone else's mouth before! Oh shit man, what a great feeling! Oh shit – oh crap, oh what can I say! Oh man, I gotta sit down! I gotta sit down!"

As Darrell was stating that his legs were about to give out and he needed to sit down someplace, Tom pulled off of Darrell's cum covered rod, wiped the sides of his mouth with the back of his hand, and said, "Well, I hope that was good cum going down my throat, since it was so fucking far back in my throat, I never tasted it! Shit man, I'm glad I told you guys to give me oxygen if I needed it, cause I have never had a dick stuck down inside of my throat as far as that one was! We sure as hell don't need to compare dicks now – I bow to the king of lengths! Darrell, how in the hell do you keep that thing hidden! No wonder I never got to see it that day in the restroom! Man, how in the hell can your wife take that!"

"How in the hell can his wife take that!" Jay almost screamed! "Didn't I tell you he had that fucker up in my ass earlier today?! He had that whole damned thing up inside of me!"

"Well, no wonder you got such a happy smile on your face man! How's your ass feeling? Feeling pretty good?"

"Yeah, man, damn good! It's feeling damn good! I was scared to hell before it happened, but Stan kept telling me it'd be OK, and it was! Man, was it! He got that up in me, and right away I knew why you gay guys do it! Shit man, I was pissed at myself, and still am, that I hadn't been doing that for years now! Tom, about how many times you been fucked in that ass? Got any idea?"

Grinning, Tom looked at Jay and replied, "Well, never really thought about that any. Hey – maybe couple hundred times a year since I was bout seventeen or eighteen, so maybe about two thousand times, give or take a guy or two! Hell, never thought about it, but, not so often when I was younger – but just as often as possible once I got a little older and could find some eager guys that needed to blow a wad or two! Hey, when I was in college, I was the town's gay whore on campus. If you had a dick, I had an ass! Why in the hell am I telling you guys this? Guess – the thinking back – well it's fun! Yeah – probably about that! Yeah. Probably couple of thousand. Most of 'em, were repeats. Either I really liked what they had as a tool, or they really liked what I had for 'em to stick their dick into! Now – having Bobby in the house, well – now, every night unless he's on the road, and then we make up for lost time when he gets back. He was gone once for four nights, and that weekend, I got it in the ass five times in one day! We ran around naked the whole weekend, and hell I could have been standing at the kitchen sink, and all of a sudden I had a dick up in my ass! Believe me guys, did not bitch about that once, either! He loves to fuck me, and I gotta admit, I love it too! Now you talk about a dick! Typical muscular black man, with the typical yardstick for a dick, but of course a hell of a lot thicker, and a hell of a lot stiffer!"

"Hey men!" Tom, then stated, to the other three that were all glowing in their respective glory from that activity that they had just accomplished. "The time is definitely marching on, and unless we're gonna involve the other three guys and tell 'em just what's going on in here, I think we better get ready for cocktail hour and some supper. I think we all kinda need to shower down again, and then maybe think about, maybe, resuming this later after the others crash out for the night? What do you guys think?"

Jay looked at Stan and Darrell, grinned, and asked, "Hey guys! Ok with you two? I sure want to! I'm definitely into this! But hey, Tom! What about you? You need to meet your man someplace tonight?"

"No. Bobby's not close by tonight! He's on the other side of the state, so I'm game if you guys are! Everybody wanna? I sure as the hell do! I need my ass fucked, and I think getting fucked by a couple of my married co-workers and a university coach will just about make my day! Hey, a good four-way! I haven't been in a four-way in months!"

"A four-way? Jay rather timidly asked. "All four of us playing with each other, all at the same time? Oh shit man, I've never done that – well of course! Oh crap man, do we really need to go to supper? I'm gonna have a raging hard on thinking about that the whole supper time! Shit man, I'm not sure I've got any pants loose enough for that! Damn, I'm gonna be showing a major hard on the entire time, I'm sure! Oh God man, I'm gonna get fucked in the ole butt hole some more – ain't I?"

Chapter Five:
"Hey What's Up?"

"Hey Tom! While we're just sitting here waiting on those other guys to turn out their lights, now that we've finally found out about the 'real you,' why don't you tell us how you and Bob met? That'll give us all something to do, while we just sit here and wait on those other three to turn out their lights, so we can all hit the hay and teach me some more stuff," Jay suggested, since the four were now waiting for the lights in the other cabin to be turned off – just as a security – so that none of the other three men would happen to come wondering in, just as the sex action got started up and going strong again.

Stan and Darrell agreed that would be a good move, since all of them were getting rather anxious for getting things started again, and the just sitting, and trying to think of things to talk about, was getting kinda of rough.

"Well, nothing real exciting, I guess, but do gotta admit it was kinda different than the way most guys meet!" Tom replied to Jay's request. "I was still at State and one night I was on my way back to my apartment, and I noticed somebody was following me, or so I thought! I was walking, and every few steps, I'd stop, turn around and some guy – Bob, would stop and

try to act as if he wasn't there. After about the third time, I finally walked
back toward him and asked."

"Hey what's up?"

"Nothing man, nothing"

"Well, what's going on then? You been following me for the last five
minutes or so, and every time I stop, so do you – and then you try to act as
if nothing was going on. What's up?"

"Hey man, don't be mad at me, OK? I didn't mean anything. I'm
sorry!"

"Yeah, but what you up to? What's going on?"

"Uh, uh. Hey, I saw you coming out of that bar, and I think I know
what that bar is. It's a gay bar right?"

"Yeah, yeah, it's a gay bar. Yeah, I'm a gay guy! So what's the big
deal? I don't understand yet what in the hell is going on!"

"Hey man, please don't be pissed at me, please! I've never been with
a guy before, and man, when I saw you, I just had to see if there was any
way I could maybe meet you. Please don't be mad!"

"Hey what in the hell are you talking about man! Why in the hell
would I wanna be mad at you? Look at you! You are one hot fucking stud!
Why in the hell would that make me mad? Hey man, just talking to some
guy, that don't mean you're gonna 'be with me." There's no harm in talking
to some guy, even if he is gay! Just cause I'm gay, that don't mean it's illegal
to talk to me, or that you've done anything wrong! Come on, let's walk.
I'm Tom Schroder!" Tom stated as he stepped one or two steps closer to the
man of muscle, so that he could extend his hand out for a hand shake with
the man that he had just "happened to meet," in a rather unusual and a very
awkward way. "Thanks man, I'm Bob Woodward."

"Thanks man!" Bob expressed as he accepted Bob's hand shake offer.

"Hey Bob, let's walk some here and let you calm down some, OK?"

"Yeah, thanks man, thanks!"

"So Bob! Never been with a guy, right?"

"Yeah! Right!"

"I rather guess maybe – you are – ah – maybe wanting to – I assume?"

"Oh man, oh man! I don't know, I don't know! Tom, I really just don't
know!"

"Wait a minute man, wait a minute! How long and how often you been hanging out, outside of the Rod Bar? Obviously you've been kinda keeping an eye open there, right?"

"No, no. Well, yeah and no! Oh Tom, I'm feeling so confused. I am! Tom, I knew that was a gay bar, but I really didn't just hang out there watching guys, but I just happened to be going down the street on the other side when I saw you come out, and all of a sudden, I got this real funny rushing feeling. All of a sudden, I wanted to be with you! I felt like I had to talk to you and maybe get to touch you. I feel like you're kind of part of me that I lost someplace. Oh shit man, shit! I know this sounds so fucking stupid. I'm so sorry, I really am! Maybe I just need to go and leave you alone!"

"Don't you dare Bob, don't you dare! Don't you dare turn around and walk away! If you really wanna see me get pissed, that would do it! Believe me man, believe me!"

"But Tom, this is way too weird, way too weird!"

"What's too weird, what? What in the hell are you talking about?"

"Me – following you like some little puppy wanting petted! Tom, you're a guy, I'm a guy! I shouldn't be trying to follow you like that! That was wrong, but at the time, I really couldn't think about doing anything else. May I touch your arm – please? Just kind of lay my hand on you for a minute?"

"Hell yes you can! Please do! I wanna feel your arm too! OK?"

"Oh yeah, oh yeah! Oh yeah man, that would be nice, really nice!"

"Hey Bob, you are one fucking hunk! You got muscles all over you in places I'm not even sure we all have! Feeling you is a hell of a lot better for me, than you feeling me, I'm sure! You are one fucking hot man, fucking hot! God man, your skin is so fucking tight and so solid! Bob, you've had other guys feel you haven't you? Other guys have rubbed their hands up and down your arms or back or someplace, haven't they?"

"No. No Tom, no! I guess I've always wanted 'em to, but nobody ever has. I guess they were afraid it would piss me off or something, and yeah, I've wanted someone to do that for a long time! Oh, I love feeling your skin! I mean it man – I like this! Thanks for letting me do this!"

As Bob and Tom stood there on the sidewalk, in the shade of a large tree blocking the direct light from the street light, they each slid their hands up and back down the length of each other's upper arms. Tom did admit that he had more muscles to feel and worship, than Bob had available to feel.

"My God man, your arms are enormous, fucking enormous!" Tom emphatically stated as he forced himself from leaning over and licking the top of, the bottom of and the pits of both of Bob's massive, muscular arms.

Slowly removing his hands from Bob's arms and his biceps, Tom looked at Bob, and asked. "You married? You got a wife?"

"No, no! No wife, got a girlfriend, but not a wife!"

"So you and your girlfriend, pretty close?"

"Man, I don't know. I just don't know."

"Well, wait a minute here man, why not? You gotta know if you're close with her or not, don't you?"

"I don't know man, I just don't know. I used to think we were close, but I just don't know anymore. She's fun to be with, but I guess I'm the one that's kind of cooling it some. I know she keeps wondering why I'm kind of, as she calls it – so distant – and I'm not sure why, but it's just not the same as when we were younger and fooling around all the time. It's just different!"

"So Bob, how old are you?"

"I'm twenty three. She's twenty."

"So how long you two been together?"

"Uh, like about four years, I guess. Yeah, I think I was like eighteen or nineteen when we met. It was fun back then, but now, it's just not so much fun, and it's not like I'm going with some other chick, it's just different. Being with her ain't nothing like what I'm feeling right now, and that's what's so weird. This is weird, but man, I took one look at you coming out of that bar, and I wanted to just cry, I'm serious man, I know that is stupid, but man, I wanted my whole life to be what it was right then. I could have gotten myself shot or beaten up or something for following you like that, but man, I really didn't care right them, I didn't. Thanks for understanding man, I really appreciate it! I know it's weird, real weird!"

Taking Bob buy the upper arm, which he wanted to feel again anyway, Tom turned him toward himself, looked him straight in the face and stated, "Bob – stop the talk about weird! It is not weird! Different than what you are used to, but not weird! Tonight you just happened to be in the right place at the right time to finally get a chance to talk to someone that you just internally knew you could talk to! Do not say weird, one more time! Understand?"

"Yeah I do! Yeah! I'm sorry, I am! Hey, I think maybe I've kind of goofed up enough of your night already! I think maybe I'll just let you go and head home. I'm sorry I screwed up your night with this crap! Thanks man, I appreciate you, I really do!"

With his hand still firmly placed on Bob's bicep, Tom strongly and emphatically stated, in no uncertain terms, "You are not going anywhere man, nowhere! Understand? There are special days in our lives when we need somebody around us, and tonight is the night that you need me! You're not going anywhere, understand?"

"Yeah, but man, I've already messed up your night, and I don't wanna be any more bother to you!"

"Stop it, end it, that's it! You are not a bother! Bob, what you aren't taking into consideration here is – if I had seen you someplace, I'm the one that would be doing whatever necessary to get a chance to talk to you! So all that's happened is – you saved me the trouble of trying to figure out some cool way of getting you to notice me so I could talk to you!"

Without saying a word, Bob quit hanging his head, as he had been doing, looked up directly at Tom, and broke a slight, smile.

"There! That's better, a lot better! Now I assume you were walking, or have you got a car someplace?"

"No, I was walking. I was feeling kind of shitty and just decided to go out and be by myself and go for a walk."

"Where you live?" Tom asked wondering just how far Bob had walked.

"Oh, over by Fourth and Simpson Lane."

"Fourth and Simpson Lane!? Tom very emphatically asked. "Bob, that is probably three miles from here! Just out walking, just walking? Is that right?"

"Yeah, I didn't wanna be home, so I just started and ended up here."

"OK man, just out walking! When you left the house, did you know where you were headed? You knew the Rod Bar was a gay bar, right? Think maybe, kinda – unconsciously, you actually wanted to – maybe – just happen, to be walking by? Think that's possible?"

Looking at Tom, Bob grinned a slight grin, and admitted, "You know man, you might be right. I really don't know! Once I was there, looking at it from across the street, I did wonder if I had automatically headed this way, not really knowing why, but unconsciously, I was hoping to find someone I could talk to. I know man, I really did want to just get a chance to feel some guy, and let that guy feel me back, just like we did! Oh yeah, I know I wanted that! I wondered about it, if I kinda headed here without really knowing it, and now of course I'm wondering why. I really don't know, I just don't! I know, I really did not know I was headed here on purpose, though!"

"Ok we don't know, and maybe we're not supposed to know, but at least the walk didn't turn out to be a bust. You met me, and I met you! And in my mind, that's pretty damn good! You have Saturdays off, or do you have to go to work tomorrow morning?"

"No, I have it off. I'm a salesman for lumber company, so I have Saturdays and Sundays off. I have to travel a lot, but this week and next week I'm in the office, so I don't have to travel. Why?"

"Why!? Why!? The why, is because since you are about three or four miles from home, I want you to stay at my place so we can do some more talking, and then you can go home when the busses are running. I don't have a car, so I can't offer you a ride."

"Oh shit man, I can't do that! Thanks, but I can't do that!"

"Why not? Afraid of me or something?"

Looking over at Tom with a very strong quizzed expression on his face, he answered, "No! No, why should I be afraid of you? No, it's just that I've already screwed up your night enough! I'll call a cab and get a ride home!"

"Sir, you did not walk for like three or four miles just to finally tell some guy that – now you need to go home. For the last time – you are not messing up my night at all. In fact, the reason I was at the bar was boredom, and nothing exciting to do, so having you with me now is definitely an upper! I am totally serious man, I do want you to stay at my place so we can talk some more! Gotta admit, I'm a university student, limited bucks, so I have a studio apartment that – yes – only has one bed in it, but I can be a good boy for one night, and promise you I will not do anything to you – unless you want me to, that is! OK? Understand? Please don't give me anymore of this shit about bothering me! Hell man, until we met, this was the night of total boredom, and now it's fun and exciting!"

"Tom, I still feel funny – oh shit man – yeah – yeah – I'll stay! I like you, you're nice to me and yeah, I really don't want to be by myself tonight, so yeah, I'll stay but I don't want to imply that I wanna do some funny stuff, OK? I mean man, I like you, but if you want me to stay just cause you think maybe I'll so some of your type of stuff ——."

"Hey guy, my type of stuff is eating something, drinking something, watching something goofy on the ole TV and some good talking. That's what my type of stuff is, OK?"

"Ok, Ok! Tom, thanks man, thanks! I gotta admit, I'm kinda glad you're kinda forcing me to stay. I want to, I really do! I just needed to let you know I knew I was intruding, and in a real big way!"

"Hey big deal! Big deal! We'll take a left turn up here at the corner, and then one short block, and we're home! Hell of a lot closer than walking to your place, right?"

Tom and Bob continued their conversation on a slightly brighter level now that Bob finally conceded to spend the night, and as they walked they each discovered more and more detail about the other guy. Bob did ask and found out that Tom was two years younger than himself, and that he would be graduating in May with a degree from computer science.

The evening was well spent getting to know a little more about each other, and watching some rather uninteresting TV. For each man, the talking and the getting to know more, was the important thing.

"Hey man, leave 'em! Just put 'em on the counter and I'll clean 'em up in the morning! Come on man, time to put the ole bodies to bed! Oh my God man – look at the time! Shit man, it's almost two thirty! I had no idea we sat and talked that long! My God man, we've been home for what, four hours? Bob, I thought it was probably only about midnight! Shit man, this has been fun!"

"Tom, I gotta tell you, I'm thanking the heavens above, for you walking out of that bar right when you did! Seriously man, I hadn't been just standing over there across the street watching the bar. I was really just walking by, and you came out! What timing!"

"Let me tell you something! We gotta thank little ole Jack Osborne for me walking out when I did. If he had shown up when he was supposed to, I would have been sitting in there drinking instead of coming out. He never showed up, and so I decided to just leave, since I was kinda getting a little provoked that he never showed up."

"So what were you guys gonna do? Just do some drinking?"

"No! If you're gonna ask – we were gonna do some fucking! He loves for me to fuck his ass, and of course, as tight as it is, I love to do it, so that's what we were planning, but then he never showed, so –what can I say?"

"So Tom, can I ask you some questions about you and other guys having sex together?"

"Yeah, hell yeah man! Of course!"

"So you were gonna fuck him, right?"

"Yeah, he might have fucked me before the session was over, but yeah, I definitely was gonna fuck him."

"So, do you usually do the fucking, or, well – I guess what happens? I know stupid question, but I've never talked to some guy about him having sex with some other guy. You don't mind do you?"

"No, hell no I don't mind! I was kind of hoping maybe we'd get into these conversations earlier, but I guess the eating and the TV kinda dictated our conversation, so no, I sure don't mind. I've got a big dick, and some guys love to feel it up in their asses, but some guys look at it and they get too scared to stick that much up in there, I guess it's kinda just who I'm with!"

"You got a big dick? Hey, can I see it? I noticed you didn't take your briefs off, so – course now that's made me wonder just what you're hiding. Can I see it? You mind? I don't wanna do anything with it, I just wanna see it, OK?"

"Hell yeah you can see it, and I wanna see yours too. I didn't take my briefs off cause you didn't either! I was waiting for you to strip down all the way, but then when you didn't, I thought maybe I shouldn't. I didn't want you thinking I was gonna try anything with you especially since I promised you earlier that I could be good for one night! I like you as a friend, and I don't wanna scare you off any. I'm gonna open these curtains a little so we've got some light in here if were' gonna compare sticks, OK?"

Tom got up and slightly opened the curtains just enough to get some light into the dark room, and as he was up, he took his briefs off. He was now supporting a partial, and growing, hard on! The talk about looking at each other's dicks had gotten him a little started. Regardless of – if it was gonna be a big dick, or a small dick, Tom was always on the ready to inspect some other guy's dick!

As he turned to get back in bed, Bob saw his rod and stated, "Oh shit man, you do have a big rod, don't you?"

Just as he stated that, Tom then saw what Bob had uncovered, by stripping off his briefs, and he emphatically and shockingly stated, "My God man! Don't make comments about mine! Look at that fucking log you've got! Oh Bob, you've got an unbelievable cock! Oh my God man, you're uncut! Oh man, I love uncut dicks! Hey man, I gotta feel that one! Oh man, let me lick it – please! Oh man, I wanna lick your foreskin! I wanna stick my tongue under your foreskin! Can I chew on that skin? Oh shit man, what a fucking boner! My God man, you've got just about the biggest cock I've ever seen and I can tell it ain't even totally hard yet, is it? Oh shit, look at that skin stretch! Oh yeah, I like this!"

As Tom was in shock and awe, and was getting more and more excited about what Bob was now showing, it was getting longer and stiffer as he reached out to touch it.

"Oh Tom – Tom, no guy's ever touched it before! You gonna touch it? Oh man, it's getting so fucking hard! Oh man, oh Tom, this is really something different for me!"

Tom reached forward, took ahold of Bob's oversized rod, first slid his tongue and then his finger up and under the foreskin, and then found out he couldn't close his hand around the shaft. "Oh my God Bob, this thing is enormous! It is fucking enormous!"

Just as he finished his statement of how thick it was, Tom made no effort to ask if he could put it in his mouth. All of a sudden, he bent over, opened his mouth, as widely as he possibly could, and threw his mouth onto Bob's hard rod. He slid his tongue up and under the foreskin and ran it around the entire circumference of Bob's dick!

"Oh my God man, oh my God! You're putting my dick in your mouth! Oh man, oh man – oh I've never had that done before! Oh Tom, you sure you wanna suck on my dick? Oh man, oh shit man, I can't believe this! Oh man, I can't believe you've got your mouth on my dick! Oh this is so weird! Oh, that's feeling good, yeah, that's feeling good to me! Oh Tom, yeah, I like that, I like that! Oh man, you've got my dick in your mouth and you're sucking on it! Oh I never thought that I'd ever have that happen! Oh man, I like this!"

Without even answering Bob's question about, did Tom really want to suck on his dick, Tom forced as much dick down, into his throat, as he possibly could. He started sucking on the part of that dick that he could get into his mouth, for two reasons! One, he loved what he was doing and the enormous oversized, big, thick, dick that he was doing it to, and number two, he wanted this to be the greatest feeling that Bob had ever had, so that Bob would be begging him, to keep it up, and not stop!

Bob threw himself back onto the bed and thrust the midsection of his body up toward Tom, not realizing that he was actually begging for this other man, to take as much of his dick down into his mouth, as he possibly could! He was flipping his head back and forth, uttering, "Yeah man, yeah! Oh yeah, oh yeah, that feels so good, yeah man I like that! Yeah, suck me man, suck me, I like that!!!"

Totally unaware of it, he reacted as any man does when he is getting a great blow job! As he was almost out of the mental conscious state of being, enjoying the unbelievable feeling of what was happening to him at that moment – he grabbed a hold of each side of Tom's head and tried to pull him on even farther!

He was getting his very first feeling of how great a hot mouth can feel on a hot dick, and he was almost "out of it" mentally celebrating internally about his great new feelings of being used by another man, and at the same time, offering himself to that man!

As Tom used every force possible, to get just as much of that big, thick, dick down into his throat, and so totally, his thrill and joy of the struggle of forcing more and more of it in, Bob was twisting and turning, flipping and jumping, on his back, all a very normal, out of self-control reaction, to the feelings that Tom was giving to not only his dick, but his total being. Bob was unconscious to all and everything, except to what was happening to him, his body, his dick, his emotions, and his total existence of being in bed, and under the total control of this hunk of a man, and letting that hunk of a man, suck on him, and use parts of himself, for an unbelievable sexual experience! An unbelievable sexual experience, for both of the men!

"Suck me man, suck me! Oh Tom, Tom suck me! Oh my God it is so fucking stiff and hard! I've never had a hard on like this! Oh man, suck on my dick!"

All of a sudden, Tom pulled off of – what he had been thinking of and mentally calling, a telephone pole, and he begged, "Oh Bob, please, please fuck me with that! Bob I need to feel that up in my ass! Bob, guys are always telling me how good my dick feels up in their butts, but I never get fucked with a big dick like that! Oh Bob, please, please – will you please fuck me!? Please!"

Trying to rather snap out of his mental state of almost unconscious bliss, and realize that Tom was talking to him, Bob responded, "Hey man, if you really want it, I guess so, but I gotta tell you, I've never fucked some guy's ass before, so you may have to tell me what to do! Seriously man, I've never done this, but if you wanna, I'll try!"

"Oh God yes man, oh God yes! Oh Bob, I've got to take that up in my butt! I've got to feel that up inside of me. Hey man, all you gotta do is find my asshole and push it up in me! OK? Please? Please tell me you'll fuck me, man, please say yes!"

"Yeah, yeah I'd do it. Tell me what to do. What do I do?"

Tom grabbed the tube of KY jelly from in the night stand, squirted a good glob up in his ass and wiped his hand on Bob's rod, and told Bob, "Hey man, I'm gonna just lay down here on my gut, you get on my butt and let your fucking big pole find my asshole and then just start pushing it in. Go kind of slow getting in at first. Let it get my ole hole opened up some, and then after you've got it in, I want all of it and I'll want it fast! Oh Bob,

I can't believe this! Oh man, I want that dick up in me and I want all of it! I want you to spread my ass far enough to make me take all of it! Oh fuck me, man, fuck me! Oh God I can't believe this! Man I want you up in me, and then I want you to shoot off in me! I want you in me! Yeah man, find my hole! Yeah, yeah! Oh go slow – oh go slow! Oh shit man, that feels like a fucking football going up I my ass man, it is so fucking big! Oh yeah, just go slow for a minute! Real slow! Let me try and relax my ass so you can go up in there! Yeah, slow, yeah real slow! Oh Bob, yeah, it's going in, it's going in! Oh yeah, oh yeah! Yeah! Oh yeah man! Oh God it's in me man – it's in me! Push! Yeah push! Yeah, go on in me, bury that dick in me man – yeah, do it, do it! Oh Bob, oh man my ass is getting so full! Oh this is great! How you doing man, how you doing? You OK?"

"Oh fuck shit yeah man, hell yes! Oh man I never thought fucking some guy's ass could feel like this! Oh shit man, your ass is so fucking tight, it is so fucking tight! Can I push some more? Can I push in some more? Oh man, your ass is hot man, hot! Oh God man – you OK? You OK? I'm not hurting you any, am I? You OK?"

"Hey man, push it all in! Give me all of it! Let me taste it up in my mouth! Let me have it! Oh man, what a great feeling! Oh Bob, I love this! I am OK man, I am OK! This is heaven man, true heaven!"

As Bob was pushing onto Tom's ass as strongly and as firmly as he could, he told Tom, "That's it man, that's it! That's all I got! I'm in as far as I can go! You like it? You like me and my big black, thick, stiff, dick up in that ass? This feel good to you? You like that? You feel it up in there, man?"

"Oh hell yes man, hell yes! It feels good and hell yes, shit yes, I like having that big black cock of yours up in there! My ass really needs that up in there! It feels good, damn good! Fuck me man, fuck me! Oh thank God Jack didn't show up tonight! Oh hell man – I'd sure have never had this dick up in me, if that little peter had showed up! Oh man I thought I was pissed at him for standing me up, and oh God, am I glad now! Bob, ram me! Slam my ass! You've got me all good and opened and you've got it all the way up in me, so now fuck the hell out of me! Let me know I've got me a man, a real man up in me, back there! Fuck me like you're punching your ole punching bag! Slam my ass good and hard! Yeah, yeah! Oh yeah! Do it!! Do it!!! Yeah keep it up – keep it up – keep it up!!! Oh man, I love it – I love it! Do me, fuck me like a fucking wild pig! Fuck my ass! Oh Bob, this is the best I've ever had man, it's the best! You like it, you like fucking this little black ass? You like it?"

Almost to the point of exhaustion, Bob did manage to utter back, "Oh hell yeah man, hell yeah! Your little black ass is making my big black dick hotter than hell man, hotter than hell! I'm getting real close to cummmin man, I'm getting real close! You want me to keep fucking you till I cum? You want me to shoot my stuff in you?"

"Oh hell yes man, hell yes! You keep it up until you totally collapse that hot sweaty muscled body on me and can't move! I wanna feel all those muscles laying on me and sweating on me! Fuck the hell out of me until you can't move anymore! Drill me, pump me, slam me, drive it in me man, drive it in me! Make me think I've got a whole fucking water tower pushed up in my ass, and it's just about to break open. Yeah – oh yeah – oh yeah – oh yeah I feel it man! I feel it!! Pump me man, pump me, pump me!! Flood me, flood me!! Give me your cum man – give me your cum! Oh Bob – oh Bob!!! Oh man, lay down on me, lay down! Yeah, just lay there, yeah lay there! Yeah, I wanna feel you and all your muscles laying on me – lay there and keep pushing it in! Oh thank God! Oh man, oh! Oh Bob, this is fucking heaven, you OK? You OK?"

"Oh hell yeah man, hell yeah – I'm OK! Tom, I think I'm more than OK! Oh shit man – that was great! Fucking great! Oh Tom, from the way that felt to me, I can't even imagine what in the hell it feels like, to be the one getting fucked! Oh Tom, will you fuck me now? Oh man, I loved it when you kept begging for me to get rougher and rougher on you! Oh please, I wanna see what it feels like to have your big dick up in my ass! Oh Tom, thank God man – you came out of that bar when you did! Oh Tom, I think this has changed my life forever – I really do!"

"And guys, it did! For him and me both! It took Bob about six or seven months of doing the girl thing and the "me thing," all at the same time, but then he finally leveled with her, and after he came running over to my place to tell me what he did, we fucked each other for the entire night and the entire next day too – and have been doing that ever since!"

"Fucking shit man, fucking shit!" Stan firmly and enthusiastically stated as Tom finished telling them about the first fucks that he and Bob had together. "Come on guys, come on! My God, after listening to Tom telling us about his first night with Bob, I'm so fucking horny now that I don't really care if somebody walks in on us or not, I need dick! Who's gonna fuck me? Come on men, I need a dick, and I need a dick now!!!"

Grinning broadly, Darrell stood up, rubbed his now obvious hard on, and said, "I'm game man, I'm game! Shit after that, I'm ready for fucking all of you guys! God Tom, you have got me so fucking hot and horny, I'm about ready to bust a nut standing here right now!"

"Shut the lights down guys!" Jay stated, as he too stood up, grabbed his now showing, through the pants, hard on, and continued, "It's time we all hit the hay and see who can fuck the longest and the hardest! Tom, you're my fucker to get started! I want you on top of me and in me! I need that dick of yours, just like you needed that dick of Bob's! I need fucked, and I need fucked good and strong! Tom listening to you tell how you and Bob first did it, it has got me all worked up! God, I'm horny men, I'm fucking horny!"

Chapter Six:
Is Some Funny Stuff Going On?

"Hey Jay, wanna ask you something." Sidney, or as commonly referred to, Sid, told Jay as they were alone and walking back toward the cabins, after the Thursday afternoon classroom session.

"Yeah, what Sid?"

"Not so sure just how to ask this, but, that Stan guy that's you guys have been kinda hanging around with the last couple of day, tell me bout him."

"Tell you bout him? What do you mean? What do you mean Sid? Tell you what?"

"He's a coach or something right?"

"Yeah, he is. Why?"

"You know much about him?"

"Well no, probably not much! Why? What's the big question here? What's going on?"

"I don't know Jay, maybe I oughta just not say anything. Just kinda forget I mentioned him, OK?"

"No Sid, no! You wanna either say something or ask something, so do it! What is it? Hey man, remember this is an Inter-Relationship training meeting we're at, so let's inter-relationship and tell me what's on your mind. OK?"

Turning toward Jay slightly, and lowering his voice some, Sid finally said, "Jay, I saw him doing some funny stuff in one of the restrooms this morning. He did not see me, and I ducked out right away, but Jay – he was doing something with some guy in there."

Now rather rattled some, Jay turned toward Sid and asked, "What? Sid, what was he doing!?"

"Jay, he was sucking on some guy. He was sucking on some guy's dick! Jay, I know he's stayed over in your guys' cabin the last couple of nights! Well, anyway, he's stayed there pretty late at night, and after you guys turned all your lights off! Jay, is some funny stuff going on over there?"

"Oh shit guy, damn! Sid, honestly man, you gotta keep this to yourself! Understand!? Damn man, I had no idea anybody else knew what was going on! Sid, do not tell anybody – do you understand?"

"Jay, trust me man, trust me! I wouldn't have asked you if I hadn't kinda known something was going on, and I wanted to find out about it. Honestly Jay, I will not say a word!"

Looking around some, and then finding a bench just a few feet away, Jay then said, "Come here Sid, come here."

Jay and Sid then sat down on the bench and Jay said, "Yes Sid, yes some stuff is going on at our cabin. Stan approached me Monday while we were both taking a shower over at the beach shower spot, and one thing lead to another, and yes, he and I ended up at the cabin and he taught me some stuff. He apparently, from what he says, plays with his football players a lot, and he just plain out and out told me he wanted to play with me, and since I'd never done anything like that, I finally, after quite a bit of encouragement, I finally agreed to it. I will be honest that at first, I was wondering if this was some funny part of making us do some new and different inter-acting between people, to teach us how to deal with other kinds of people. Well, it didn't turn out that way, but Sid, I'll tell you, now, I'm not sorry I agreed to do it!"

"Sid, I'm forty-five with two college aged daughters. I'd never done any of this stuff and when he suggested that we do it, I guess maybe I decided that at least once in my life, I needed to do the wild and different. Sid, I'm glad I did."

"Well Jay, is it just you and that Stan guy, or what about Tom and Darrell? They doing this too?"

"Yeah Sid, yeah. All of us are doing it. I guess since I and Darrell now know it, I guess it's OK to tell you that through this, we found out that Tom is gay. He has a partner, but we never knew that!"

"Oh shit! Shit!"

"Wait a minute Sid, wait! Why did you say that? Why did you say, shit?"

Kinda shaking his head and letting it lower some, Sid then replied, "Cause you just answered everything that I wanted to know! Jay, I think – I say I think, I'm gay, but I really do not know for sure. That's one of the main reasons that I asked the company to send me to this Inter-relationship meeting thing. Course I didn't tell them that, but that was the reason I asked if I could be part of it. I used other excuses. I told 'em that I thought maybe it might help me with the nasty customers that I have to deal with all of the time."

Now leaning in a little more closely to Sid and speaking in a much more confidential tone, Jay asked, "So Sid, what did I answer right there? What did you mean?"

Now really hanging his head and speaking quite quietly, Sid answered, "If he was gay, and then if he had a partner. And yes, and yes! Yeah, I finally found out he's gay, but I was hoping he didn't have a partner."

"So, I kinda guess maybe you are kinda turned on by Tom, right?"

"Hey Jay, I'm really sorry now that I even brought this up! I shouldn't have! I'm sorry, let's just forget all about it man – let's just forget it!"

"No Sid, no! Sid I don't want to! I think you have finally leveled with someone about something that is important to you, and hey, maybe this inter-relationship stuff is really paying off for you! Maybe you are picking up some stuff here that you did not even realize you were hearing. Seriously man, I'm not so sure that four or five days ago, either you or I would have been comfortable having this kind of a conversation, but look, here we are, and we're sharing stuff with each other that a few days ago we would have never had the nerve to mention. I'm a forty-five year old father of two college age daughters, and I just admitted to you, that yes, I had sex with a man. And yes, I enjoyed it! You're a what? Twenty four, twenty five year old guy that is finally telling somebody that you think you might be gay, and one hell of a hot built black man is a turn on, to you! Right? Right? Am I right Sid?"

"Yes Jay, yes! Honestly man, I have never told anybody that I thought maybe I was gay! Never! You are the first person that I ever admitted that too! And yes, I think Tom is about the hottest thing walking on the face of this earth! I've worked close to him for about two years now, and yes, Jay, I will admit I go home at night and jerk off, thinking about him and wondering what he looks like all bare and naked! I was really, really disappointed when I found out that he and I were not gonna be in the same cabin this week! I almost cried, cause I was hoping that maybe by chance, I'd get to see him going into the shower all bare and naked. Jay, has he got a really big dick?"

"Yeah Sid, yeah! He's got a nice dick, but the surprise is Darrell's! Even Tom made good comments about that one. And let's be honest, when a black man makes good comments about some white guy's dick, that means it is a good dick! Tell me Sid, how much playing around have you done? You have had gay sex before, right?"

"Oh Jay, not much, not much! I've had a few good times with some guys, but not very often."

"So Sid, what kind of guys turn you on? Tell me who you've done stuff with and tell me about 'em."

"Jay you don't want to do this! I'm sure you've got other stuff you wanna do. Hell man, maybe your Stan guy is over at your cabin waiting for you. Forget it man, come on forget it!"

"No Sid, no! I think maybe you have finally started to open up to somebody about some stuff that is important to you, and hey man, what better time than now, at a meeting designed to get this type of stuff going. Well, maybe we won't be able to go back to class and tell what we talked about, but knowing that you and I did have this kind of a conversation, should give both of us the confidence that we can do this with other people, on other subjects! Right?"

"Yeah, yeah I guess."

"OK then Sid, tell me about the most exciting time you had with some guy. Open up, tell me – ok?"

"Jay, I'm sorry I brought this up man, I am! You don't want to spend time doing this!"

"Yes I do Sid, yes I do! Hey, look at it this way man! I did not do some of this type of stuff when I was younger, so maybe I'm wanting to live some of these experiences through you, OK? Talk to me, tell me! Give me the low down! Tell me what you have done and the kind of a guy you did it with. Hey, listen, I'm not your daddy, and I'm not some minister! I'm a friend. A friend that just wants to know what you've done! OK? Tell me about the most exciting time you had with a guy, and tell me about him."

Softly, shyly and quietly, Sid said, "About three years ago, I was in Atlanta. I went into a bar. I had taken a gay directory with me. I was just sitting there drinking a beer, and this big guy came up and sat down beside me. Big black man! Older than me. I think he was thirty or thirty one. Somewhere in there! I looked over toward him, and I guess I must have had a funny expression on my face, cause he asked me if I was afraid of him. I almost screamed 'NO!' It was the just all of him! I still don't know if he had been one of those TV wrestle guys or not, but I damn near fainted when he wanted to sit beside me and talk to me. Jay, I stand like about maybe five foot ten and weigh in at probably one seventy or one seventy-five, at the most, and this guy, he had to stand at least six foot four and weigh in at two sixty or two seventy! A chest on him and a butt on him that would make any bull jealous! I mean it, I do! This was the hottest looking thing walking around Atlanta that night! He was!"

"And so ——! Did you talk to him? What happened?"

"Yeah, we talked. We were at the counter, and after we sat there for a little while and talked, then he told me he always liked guys from Philly! I knew that was a bunch of crap, but hey, I didn't care where he was from, right then all I was concerned about was that he was there beside me and talking to me! I know damn well some other guys in the bar were watching us and I know damn well some of they were wishing I'd get up and leave! I had the 'gold of the pot,' sitting right there and talking to me, and then putting his hand on my crotch! Jay, he actually moved his hand over and put it right on my crotch so the other guys could see him doing it! He wanted them to see him doing it. It made me feel like a 'king.' All of a sudden I felt like I was bigger than the big guys in there. My dick was already hard, but that made it harder and made it leak some. It got the front of my Levi's wet. Well, not a big spot, but a spot anyway."

"So Sid, what happened? Did you and he do anything?"

"Yeah, yeah! He told me he wanted me to go home with him."

"So did you? You go home with him?"

"Yeah, yeah, I didn't know if I should or not, but yeah, I did. I rode over to his place, with him in his Jeep since I didn't have a car there, and as we got out of the Jeep, he asked,"

————

'So Sid, how long you gonna be in town?'

"Two more days! Gotta go home on Saturday! You live here by yourself Thor?"

As he unlocked the side door, opening into the kitchen, Thor answered, "Yeah, just me! Used to have a roommate, but he moved out a few months ago, so now it's just me. Come on guy, come on, let's get inside and get comfortable."

Thor closed the door, opened the refrigerator, grabbed two beers, handed one to Sid, and said, "Come on man! Let's go in the living room and get comfortable."

The two men did. Thor led the way, and Sid followed. As Thor got into the living room he immediately pulled off the snow white T-shirt that had been hiding the massive chest muscles, and threw it to the side. The pure white shirt, against the dark mahogany skin had shown like a big bright movie screen in a dark theater! Beautiful, beautiful!

"Hey come on Sid, get comfortable! At least for a while, consider this 'home,' and get comfortable. Take you shirt off, and your pants too, if you want!"

As Thor said that, he then bent over and removed his shoes and socks. Wiggling his toes some, he stated, "There, that feels better!"

Then looking at Sid, Thor asked. "Not real familiar with going home with guys are you? You're acting kinda nervous! Don't do this very often do you?"

"No hell no! Thor, I gotta be honest with you man, I gotta be honest. I'm not so sure if I should be here or not! I've hardly ever done anything with a guy, I mean sexually, I haven't! But when you sat down beside me, I just wilted! I did! Do you know how fucking hot you are to a guy like me? Seriously man, you are a walking God to a guy like me! You got a beautiful body, really beautiful! You got muscles all over you – all over you!"

Looking at Sid, Thor replied, "Yeah, yeah! And now that you've noticed them, come over here and let me feel you touching 'em. Come on Sid. Get over here and rub your hands on me! I wanna feel you touching me! I might be a big old muscle boy, but without guys like you that like to feel and touch guys like me, what's the use? Come on, bring your beer and come over here and sit beside me! I wanna feel you too! I wanna rub your legs and feel that dick again that I felt at the bar. Not real small is it? I felt it getting bigger and bigger as we sat there. And did you see those three guys sitting close to us watching me grab your crotch? I think they were wanting theirs grabbed too, don't you?"

Thor patted the space beside him on the couch, indicating that as a space for Sid to move to, and Sid did.

Sid had not yet taken his shirt off, so as he sat down, Thor reached over and unbuttoned the shirt, then helped Sid take it off. As it came off, Thor leaned over and licked Sid's left nipple.

"Oh Thor, oh man, that is nice! That is nice! Oh thank you, thank you!"

And as Thor was in the process of licking and sucking on Sid's nipple, his left hand slid down Sid's chest, onto his stomach, onto his buckle, and very conveniently managed to unbuckle the belt, and also unbutton the Levi's. Much to his surprise, as he slid his hand down into the Levi's, he looked at Sid and surprisingly said, "Oh man, you don't have any shorts on do you? I didn't know that! I figured you had like boxers on when I grabbed your dick! I like that! No shorts nor briefs! You are my kind of man!"

And with that said, Thor stood up, unbuckled his belt, unbuttoned his Levi's and pushed them down and stepped out of them. Sid sat there and within only about twelve or fourteen inches, straight in front of his face, he looked at the longest, the thickest, the strongest black cock, that he had ever seen in a magazine or on a video.

"Oh my God! Oh my God that is enormous! Oh Thor, you've got an enormous dick! Thor that is a fucking log! Thor, my God man, how fucking big is that thing?"

"Ya like it – ya like it? Touch it – touch it! Yeah, yeah, oh yeah, I like that! Hey guy, lean over there and lick it. Lick it. You've licked and sucked on other guys' dicks before, haven't you?"

"No Thor, no! No man, I never have. I've just jerked off with some guys before, but Thor, I've never licked or sucked on some guy's dick."

"Never, you've never licked or sucked on another guy's dick, right?"

"No, I never have, no I haven't!"

"Okay! You wanna though? You're looking at it kinda like you wanna. Right? You wanting to lick on that?"

Looking up at Thor, Sid nervously answered, "I think! I think I do – but I've never done that before! I don't know if I can or not! I'm not sure I can do it! Thor, it's a man's dick, and it's so big! It's so fucking big it's kinda scary! I've never played with a small dick, I don't know if I can or not!"

"Sure you can, sure you can. Hey, tell you what! I'm gonna just lay down here on the couch and you sit there on the floor beside me and just kinda lean over and lick parts of me. Just run your tongue up and down my skin, and then get down there toward ole 'Major' as I call him whenever you feel like it."

Sid looked up at Thor and asked, "Major!? You call your dick Major? Is that right?"

Grinning back toward Sid, Thor answered, "Yeah! Yeah I do. That way when I wanna say something about it, I can call it Major, and people that don't know me don't know I'm talking about my boner dick! Kinda like, I can say, 'Major and I are gonna go over to the gym and see who we can run into over there.' Friends know that really means that I'm gonna go over to the club and see who I can find to run into, or, in other words – run my dick up into! See if I'd said something like I was gonna take my cock over to the club, that really wouldn't have sounded so nice. So yeah, he's 'Major!' And Major wants you to know he's there, and so that's why he's waving back and forth at you!"

Sid grinned at the comment about why Thor's dick was moving back and forth, sticking up from Thor's crotch, and he then reached over and grabbed ahold of it with both hands, and squeezed. Sid jerked it up and down, and then pulled it toward himself and let it slide up along the side of his face. He did not put his mouth on it, nor stretch his tongue out to touch it, but just seeing him slide it along the side of his face, made Thor happy.

"Yeah man, yeah! See it ain't gonna bite you any! It's just anxious for you to taste it and let you see how nice and warm it is."

Sid continued rubbing on Thor's dick and continued to move it back and forth, and again and again, let it slide up along the side of his face.

Thor laid there, with his hands up above his head and said, "Yeah man, yeah. Sid I know you wanna lick me don't you? Come on man, lean over there and lick my chest and suck on my tit! I love to have my tits sucked on man, I love it. Lean over here and take that tit in your mouth, and watch my dick jerk back and forth when you do that! My tits and my dick are connected together! You lick on a tit, and my ole dick gets all excited. Real excited! It jumps back and forth when you lick on my tits! It's like an electrical charge right down to my dick!"

Sid reached up higher, he got up on his knees so that he was now a little higher up above Thor, and he did take Thor's left nipple into his mouth, and as he watched down to watch Thor's cock, he sucked on that nipple, and then slightly bit onto it. Thor's dick did jump back and forth, and up and down. It looked like a flag pole out in the middle of a category four hurricane. It moved and swayed back and forth, but it still stood there!"

"Slap it Sid, slap it! Yeah man, yeah! It loves to be slapped around and pushed back and forth! Yeah man, yeah! Yeah, slap it hard, yeah really slap it! Don't be afraid of it, yeah, really slap it! Yeah Sid, I like that – that feels good!"

Sid was starting to get a little more comfortable in touching Thor's body, and his much more private spots. He knelt there on his knees beside the couch and of course beside Thor, and continued to play around with Thor's massive rod, and also slide his hands up and down Thor's body. His left hand moved down and slid down beside Thor's cock and bag of nuts. Sid looked up at Thor and asked, "Can I grab your nuts? Can I feel 'em?"

"Oh God yes man, hell yes! Come on man, I wanna feel you grabbing my nuts man, I wanna feel that! Grab 'em tight!"

Sid laid his right hand on Thor's chest and slightly pinched his right tit, and at the same time, slid his left hand down below 'Major,' as Thor called it, and then grabbed onto the bag of nuts!

"Oh Thor – oh Thor! Oh man, you've got big nuts! Your nuts feel really big!"

With that statement, Sid moved down to where he could move Major over out of the way, and he pulled the bag of nuts up as far as possible so that he could see them. He separated the left nut from the right nut and stretched the skin around it.

"Oh man! Thor, this nut is about as big as a golf ball! Thor, it's enormous! My God man, is the other one as big? Thor, how in the hell can you wear something like swimming trunks or shorts with this much dick and this much nuts down here! Thor, I love these, I love 'em! Oh man, this is like playing with pool balls. Oh man, they feel like pool balls!"

And with that excitement and that joy, Sid did almost without thinking, throw his head right down into Thor's crotch and started licking his nuts! He licked all around the bag, which he thought was almost the size of a shopping bag, and then much to Thor's surprise, sucked his left nut up and into his mouth!

"Oh my God yes man, oh yes! Oh Sid suck it man, suck it! Suck that nut man, suck that nut!! Chew it man, chew on it! Oh yeah Sid, oh yeah! Oh man alive that feels so fucking good! Do it man, do it! Chew it, chew it! Suck it in your mouth man, suck on it – suck it tight! Suck it real tight!"

Sid really did not need any encouragement to suck that bag of nuts. Once he had his mouth down in there and starting on that nut, he immediately jumped up and got himself in position to where he could actually throw his head up between Thor's massive legs and push his head up and onto that bag of nut! The mass of muscles on Thor's legs were holding Sid's head in place as he sucked first the left nut, and then letting it slide out, sucked the right nut in, to replace it!

"Oh Sid man, Sid! Oh man I thought you told me you'd never played with some guy before! Man if you've never played with some guy before, then I wanna know what woman has got the nuts you learned how to suck on like that! Oh man, I haven't had a man suck on those nuts like that for years and years! Man that feels good, real good!"

As Thor was telling Sid of how great that nut sucking felt to him, Sid did try to take both nuts into his mouth at the same time, but the truth is, two cantaloupes cannot fit into one candy wrapper at the same time. Way too much nuts! Sid had to accept the fact, that one nut at a time was the limit, the absolute limit!

Pulling off of the bag for just a second, Sid looked up at Thor and asked, "Any guy ever had both of these nuts in his mouth at the same time?"

Thor looked down and replied, "No! No. But I will tell you that one time I thought one guy was gonna bite one in two just trying. He was damned determined that he was gonna do it, and I thought I was gonna have one big nut and two smaller nuts left by the time he got done biting and chewing on 'em! I swear, I thought he was gonna bite one of 'em in two!"

Sid had gone back to chewing on the, what felt like to him, the two baseballs that Thor had packed in his bag – when all of a sudden – he pulled off, pulled the bag, and of course the big, oversized, cock up and out of the way, and pushed his face down into Thor's deep crotch, and started licking on the skin between his nut bag and his ass. Thor rather raised up some and looked down to make sure, that what he thought was happening, was actually happening. It was! He was getting a good deep licking. He attempted to pull his mid-section up some, so that if Sid was trying to get to his asshole, he could, but getting up far enough just did not work. He rested back down and enjoyed the very unexpected deep licking and feeling that Sid was doing to him, at him, and on him! Mouth, tongue, hands and fingers everywhere!

'Oh my God!" Thor thought to himself. "Oh my God, he's got some fingers up in my ass! He is actually finger fucking me! This man is one hell more of a man and a player, than I thought he was gonna be when I got him over here!'

Keeping his fingers stuck up and into Thor's ass, Sid repositioned himself so that he was now lying on top of Thor, and had his face right at Thor's belly button. He reached his tongue out, he licked the little cavity of the belly button, then slid back some and ran his tongue down the muscles of Thor's gut. Finger fucking him with one hand, reaching up and pinching his tit with the other hand, running his face and his tongue up and down Thor's body, made Sid go crazy with excitement! He could feel Major's strength and length underneath him as he moved back and forth. He raised up, he looked at Major, he looked up at Thor, Thor silently looked back but did not say anything because he rather thought he knew what was about to happen, and it did! Sid dipped down, grabbed the rod, aimed it for his mouth and took about three or four inches of it in his mouth! Thor could feel him taking big deep breaths, both around his cock, and through his nose. Thor knew Sid was almost in a state of shock, that he had actually taken part of that dick into his mouth!

Probably unconsciously, not realizing that he was even doing it, Sid wiggled the three fingers that he had stuffed up in Thor's ass. Thor could feel them moving, and he appreciated the feeling! It felt good, and of course, the whole idea that Sid had taken part of his dick into his mouth was more than just feeling good! It was exciting! Thor knew that he was giving Sid his very first dick to suck on and chew on! With the body and the looks that Thor walked around with every day, it was not hard for Thor to pickup and take home some guy, that had never done any actions with another guy. But, and the big word is, but, seldom did those occurrences start to compare with what was happening to him, on his couch right then. He had found himself one man, that yes, was new to all of this action, but one man that was a learner and a very anxious and fast learner. This time he had brought home a jewel! A diamond in the rough!

For more than a half of an hour, Thor laid there and calmly and patiently helped Sid learn how to take one of the state's largest, biggest black cocks, back into his throat – just as far as possible. After about the first five minutes of attempted sucking, Sid did pull off and ask, "Thor, can I keep trying? I know I don't know how to do this right, but man, I wanna! I sure as hell never thought that I'd ever be putting a man's dick in my mouth when I got up this morning, but Thor, I gotta know I took this one! This one is a blue ribbon dick, and I wanna play with the grand prize! Okay, can I?"

Looking down at Sid, Thor answered, "You do what you want as long as you want! When I saw you sitting there at that counter in the bar, something just told me that you were the man of the hour, the man of the day, the man of the week, and you sure are! Sid, you do whatever you want, and you take your time! Major is yours! Take care of him! Do him honors man, and do him good!"

———

"Oh my God, Sid! Sid you had that kind of an experience with a man like that, and you say you don't know if you are gay or not? Is that right?"

"Yeah Jay, yeah. He's really the only guy that I've ever done anything like that with, and I don't know if that was just something that happened or not. I'm not sure I'd do it again if something like that happened again."

"Is what maybe you're trying to tell me is – you'd kinda like to maybe do something with Tom – so see if that would be as much fun as you had with that Thor guy, right?"

"I guess, I really don't know, I don't."

"You said Thor was a black man, right?"

"Yeah, yes he was! Yeah."

"Tom is a black man, right? I mean, I know he is, but he's another black man that you are attracted to, right?"

"Yeah, yeah."

"Are there any other black men that you know that kinda turn you on?"

"Oh I don't know. Well yeah, I kinda guess maybe there is another guy."

"Who? Who is he?"

"He's like the supervisor or something for the car washing part of the service center where I take my car. They have a filling station, and car repair shop, and gift shop place and the car washing station all there, all together. He kinda takes care of the 'cars coming in' section of the car washing part."

"So tell me about him. What's he like?"

"I really don't know too much about him, but I think he looks about as sharp as any guy can look. He's about my age, petty normal built, about five feet ten or eleven, probably about one seventy or one seventy-five, and a really nice face. I think maybe I like him so much cause of his personality! He's always smiling! He always talks to me. He always has a black shirt and black pants on, and kinda of like black dress shoes. He doesn't dress like the rest of the guys there. They look like they've got uniforms on, but this guy, he's more dressed. He's always sharp as a tack! I love to watch him walk. I can't explain it, but his walk is so smooth! When he walks, it looks like he just glides. It doesn't look like he takes any steps, he just kinda glides from here to there. He's smooth man, real smooth!"

"So what do you know about him? Do you talk to him enough to know if he's a gay guy or not? Do you know?"

"No I don't know! I don't and yeah, I wish I did! I'd really like to know that he is gay, and then maybe I'd feel more comfortable talking to him some."

"So has he given you any indication that maybe he is. He done anything or said anything that maybe indicates that he might be?"

"Other than just talking, not much. When I first really started noticing him though, was earlier this year when a friend of mine, a black man, was in town and stayed with me for a couple of weeks, and when he was with me, that is when I thought he was really paying a lot more attention to us than he had before. I wondered if it was because I had a black men with me or just the why. I really don't know. I still see him, but I still don't know much about him."

"Well Sid. If this man, the car wash guy, if he did come onto you somehow, and he indicated that he really wanted to get to know you, would you let him do that? Become a friend?"

"Oh yeah, oh yeah. I think he is sharp. He'd be a good friend if possible! Yeah!"

"Well, let me take it another step. What if you found out that he wanted to have sex with you. Would you? Would you do it?"

"Oh God yes! Oh hell yes I would! In a minute!"

"Are there any white guys that you know that you feel the same way about? Any white guys that turn you on like that?"

"No, no. No, I don't know of any."

"Sid, look at the whole picture here. Big Thor turned you on in a big way, right?"

"Yeah, yeah! That big hunk, yeah!"

"Tom turns you on, don't he?"

"Oh yeah, yeah! He always has. I've always wondered if he turns me on because of my goofing around with Thor before that. I thought maybe I was trying to make Tom, become Thor, for me. He's a different guy, I know, but I just thought since they were kinda similar, I was hoping to relive that night I spent with Thor, with Tom."

"And this car wash guy, he's black too – right? You said he was black right?"

"Yeah he is, yeah. You know what Jay? I kinda think maybe I see what you're headed for here man. I don't know if I'm gay or not, only because it's just the black men that turn me on – right?"

"Yeah Sid, yeah! I think so! Black men are hot to you, and the white guys – well just not your style – but yes, you do like black men, and in my mind, there is nothing wrong with that! Some guys only like blonde babes, some guys only like the heavier women, and some guys only like the babes that have to have a walker to help keep 'em up right and not fall over forward with their big boobies! You like black man, and I say – go for it man – go for it! You agree? Think maybe that is part of your confusion? Be gay! Don't fight it, just go for it, but just know the black guys are your cup of tea! Hey, Sid, know what you might do?"

"Uh what? What?"

"I think you ought to be open and up front with Tom, and tell him you are gay, and you have now realized that it's the black men that you like, and see if he has any black friends that maybe he can introduce you to. What do you think?"

"Yeah Jay, yeah! It's time I just accept everything about me and quit trying to make things different than they are. I know I'm gay! Now I accept the fact that I'm gay. I'm just gay with some particular wants and desires. You know Jay, I'm sure you've hear the old saying, "Go black, you never go back!" I think I am a real representation of that! Thor was my first main man doing something with, and maybe because of him, maybe he is the reason I can't go back – so to say!"

"You just might have a point there! Maybe you're thinking that all guys have to be just like that one! Remember, there's no two people that are exactly the same and all alike!"

"Hey Jay, thanks man, thanks. You know sitting down with somebody and thrashing through stuff can really help a person kinda sort out their lives once in awhile. Jay, thanks for the time and the talk! I do appreciate it, I do!"

"Hey Sid, I'm glad we talked, but I've got a question now that I'd like to ask. A few minutes ago you mentioned 'that night' that you spent with Thor. You spent the night? The whole night? I didn't know that! You got some more details to tell me about that night?"

"Well not too much details, but yeah I spent the night. Wait – that was Wednesday night, and then the next night was Thursday night, and then you know Friday night comes next. Yeah, I spent the night and then two more. Kinda stupid of me ain't it?"

"Stupid of what? Staying with that guy? Is that what you're saying?"

"No – no not that! Wouldn't you kinda think that if I spent three nights in bed with some big black man that's hung as long as a yardstick, and I didn't wanna get out of bed the next morning, that I'd finally assume that yes, maybe I am gay? I've never slept over at some gals place for three nights like that! I had meetings that I had to go to on both that Thursday and Friday, so I had to go back to my hotel room each morning and night to change clothes, but he told me he wanted me to come back each night, and I did! I loved being with that guy! We had fun, I had fun! Jay, it sure as hell, has taken me a long time to finally figure myself out, ain't it? Damn I'm glad you took the time to talk to me, thank you Jay – thanks!"

"Hey guy, don't thank me! Just be glad you decided to talk to me and kinda get some stuff out to where you could see yourself a little better. You happy with what you've kinda discovered here?"

Looking over directly at Jay, Sid emphatically stated, "Yes, hell yes! You know it's always kinda hard to finally make some big major decisions about ourselves once in awhile, but I've finally made one big one today! I guess my whole life has kinda been put on hold, just waiting for something like this to happen, and for someone like you to happen along, that had the patience and understanding enough to help me work it out! I am done, absolutely done, with trying to be somebody I am not! It took this conversation but Jay, I am now ready to admit it and accept the fact that – yes, I am gay – and yes, it's the black men that turn me on!"

Reaching over some and patting Sid on the shoulder, Jay simply said, "Great man! Great! I am glad we talked. Real glad! You gonna be okay now? You okay?"

"Yeah Jay yeah! You know, the part of this whole conversation that I do think helped me the most, was when you reminded me that some guys only like blonde babes, some guys only like the heavier women, and some guys only like babes with big boobies! I really do think that helped me accept that fact, that I do not need try to fall in love, with every gay guy! If I like black men the best, so be it, accept it, and go for it! Thanks Jay!"

Chapter Seven:
The Talk With Tom

"So Sid, what's going on man, what's up?"

Sid and Tom were seated in a nice quiet corner of a local bar, or maybe it should be referred to as a Cocktail Lounge, since it was in the middle of the day, and definitely a classier place than some of the "downtown" drinking establishments. Sid had mentioned to Tom that if at all possible, he'd like to take some time and have some nice quiet conversation, if he did not mind. Thus – the quiet corner booth in the resort lounge, where conversations were not normally overheard.

"Tom, I now know of what's going on over in your cabin. I got kinda nosy and kinda kept an eye open toward it a couple of nights, and I realized that your buddy Stan was leaving really late, like well after the lights were all turned off. So anyway, I talked to Jay, and to be real honest about it, he really helped me sort some stuff out about myself. He admitted that yeah, some funny stuff, it that's what you wanna call it, was going on over there."

"Yeah, okay! Uhhh, is that okay with you or what? Why we talking about this?"

"Oh no, it's okay with me – it's okay! The reason I talked to Jay was though, ———." And with that half of a sentence stated, and unfinished, Sid dropped his head and went quiet. He just looked down at the table as if somebody else was gonna finish it for him.

"Though ——though what? Sid, what? Why did you talk to Jay?"

Looking over toward Tom, but not very strongly, Sid finally finished the sentence with, "I wanted to find out if you were gay or not! Yeah, I asked him if things were going on over there and were you part of it, and were you gay."

"Okay, okay! So you asked! What happened?"

"He told me that yes, you are gay, but yes, you do have a partner."

Now with a very big grin on his face, but yet a very confused grin, Tom leaned over toward Sid slightly and said, "Yes I'm gay and yes I have a partner, but Sid, I still do not know why we are talking about this, and if you do or do not like that I am a gay guy, I really can't care. What difference does that make to you? Why are you so interested in my life? Why?"

Now looking over at Tom, and almost with a tear in his eye, Sid managed to say, "Cause I really like you, I do! I was hoping you did not have a partner! I didn't know if you were gay or not and I gotta be honest I was really, really hoping that if you were gay, that you did not have a partner. But Jay told me that you do. I wish you didn't."

"Sid, Sid, Sid!! What are you trying to tell me here? What are you saying? Sid, are you gay? Is that what you are saying?"

"Yeah, yeah, I am. Tom I really did not really know that, or maybe just did not accept that, until Jay and I had a real long talk. He help me understand some of my real confusions about myself."

"Sid, what are you saying? What confusions? What do you mean?"

"Ever since we've been working together, I've looked at you, and looked at you, and yes, I've gone home at night and jerked off wishing you were there with me. But I just refused to think that I was a gay guy and I kept trying to ignore it, and well – that was till I wondered if you were over there in the other cabin and doing stuff with that Stan, and the other guys. When I thought that was a possibility, that was what made me talk to Jay and ask if things were happening over there. Then he told me yes, and yes you were involved, but yes, you do have a partner. That was the real heart breaker for me, it was."

"But wait a minute here! I'm getting really confused here. You're telling me that yes, you are gay, but yet you never knew if I was or not, but never tried to find out? Is that right? Is that right?"

"Yeah, yes! Tom, I was really, really disappointed when I found out that you and I were not gonna be staying in the same cabin down here. I really was hoping that we were gonna be in the same cabin cause I was really hoping that maybe, just by chance, I'd get to see you naked sometime. Like maybe going into the shower or something. Tom, I've always wanted to see you naked."

"So – so why didn't you let me know? If you thought I was gay, why didn't you talk to me? Why did you talk to Jay? He's not gay."

"Yeah I know, I know. I guess I just needed to talk to someone like him to help me sort myself out. I really did not know for sure if I was gay or not. Tom, you and other black guys get me all real hot and bothered, but white guys don't, so I wasn't sure if I was gay or not."

"Us black guys get you turned on, but white guys don't? Right? So because white guys don't excite you, is that why maybe you didn't think you were gay? Right?"

"Yeah, yeah. I know now that is stupid, but that was the way I was thinking. Like I told Jay, I've only had one really gay experience before, and that was with a guy named Thor – about three years ago down in Atlanta. He was a really, really big black man, and yes, I had so much fun with him, that I thought maybe, just maybe that I was just getting excited around black guys, just trying to maybe, relive that time I had with him. Tom, he was hot, he was fucking hot! He looked like one of those TV wrestler guys. He had muscles all over him, and yes, he had the kinda of a dick that everybody says you black guys have. It was big! I asked Jay about yours and he told me that yes, you've got a big one too. When he told me that, I just wanted to cry! I was really jealous that he was getting to see it and play with it, but I wasn't. Then he told me that Darrell has a big one, but I didn't care. On him, I just did not care, nor even want to see it. But when he told me about yours, I just wanted to wilt. Tom, can I see it sometime? Please?"

Now sitting there, with his hand under the table and grabbing his own crotch, Tom replied, "Yes, sure. Of course you can sometime Sid, of course.

All of this you're telling me today is kind of shocking, you know? I never expected you of being a gay guy. Maybe I should have been paying better attention to the people around me, right? Hey, wait a minute here man, wait a minute! Wait a minute! About a year ago! That day we were cleaning out that storage room in the office. That Saturday that some of us came in and did some cleaning up and moving furniture around some, you and I worked together in the storage room! You were kinda hot for me that day, weren't you? You remember what happened? Yeah Sid, yeah, I kind of think maybe something could have happened with us that day if I'd been paying a little more attention, wouldn't it? Oh yeah – I remember that day,——"

———

"Hey Sid, wanna help me carry these boxes down to the basement? George told me that we're gonna store this stuff down there till they decide what to do with it. Here, take these and I'll put these on this two-wheeler and take 'em."

Sid and Tom headed out of the office, down the hall and toward the elevator. Sid pushed the 'down' button, and shortly the doors opened. Tom wheeler the two-wheeler in and Sid followed with the two boxes that he was carrying. As they got into the elevator, Sid bent over to set his boxes on the floor, and as he started to stand back up, Tom looked at him and asked, "What you looking at man, what's up?"

Unfortunately Sid did take a little longer than maybe necessary to straighten back up as he definitely did take a good long notice of the bulge that was showing very nicely in the front of Tom's cutoffs.

Quickly Sid replied, "Oh nothing! Nothing! Just trying to stand back up. Those are kinda heavy."

"Oh, okay, okay. Just thought maybe you found something that you wanted to notice some more of, that's all. Just asking."

As the elevator reached the bottom floor, Tom wheeled the two-wheeler out, Sid picked up the two boxes on the floor and they headed for the far end of the basement, where their company did have some additional items stacked and stored.

Going back toward the elevator, Sid commented, "Bet the elevator is still there and waiting for us since not many people in the building today using it."

Looking over toward Sid, Tom did reply. "Oh that's too bad."

Now looking over toward Tom seriously, Sid asked, "Too bad? Why too bad?"

Just grinning broadly, Tom replied, "Oh just thought maybe we'd have to kinda just stand here for a few minutes and kinda look at each other, but guess not. Too bad!"

As the two men re-entered the waiting elevator, Tom looked over at Sid and asked, "So your back okay now? It okay?"

"Yeah, yeah. Thanks, yeah it's okay!"

Rather quietly the two men waited for the elevator to reach the eighth floor, but Tom did notice Sid glance, once or twice, to the extra girth that he was nicely showing around the mid-section of his torso. As Sid moved forward to exit the elevator, Tom again asked, "Your back okay?"

Silently Sid stepped off of the elevator, and went back into the office.

———————

"Shit man, shit! Sid, you were looking at my crotch that day weren't you? You were looking! I was right! I thought you were! Damn man, damn! And to think that Bobby was out of town on a sales trip that day – I could have had you if I'd have made the move, right?"

"Tom, I saw it, yeah I did. But I didn't know what to do, or if I should have done anything! Yeah, you were showing kinda a lot that day. That was the only day that I ever saw you in anything 'cept dress pants, and yes, all of your dress pants are way too loose and baggy on your front. They fit your ass nice, but they don't show anything on your front! Those cutoff Levi's that Saturday, those were hot as hell on you. You do have a big dick, don't you?"

"Hey man, I don't know if to say yes or no, cause you need to tell me about the big wrestler guy you played with in Atlanta. From what you've said, he sounds like he might be swinging a biggie! Does he? Can you tell me how much he's got?"

"On the second night that I was there, he measured it for me."

"Wait, wait here man! On the second night!? Second night? I thought you just had a session with him! On the second night!?"

"Oh yeah. I met him at a bar on Wednesday night, and we went over to his apartment. Then he wanted me to come back Thursday night, and then Friday night too. So yeah, I was kinda with him for those three nights. I had to leave during the days to go to the meetings I was supposed to be at, but then I went back those nights too. So yeah, I was there three nights."

Looking around to make sure that nobody had come in and sat down too close to them, Tom then leaned over slightly closer to Sid and said, "You must me one hot fucker in bed if you got to spend three nights in bed with some guy that looked like one of the big guys on TV wrestling. Those are big boys! So tell me, he measured it for you. Don't tell me that he had never measured it before! Did he tell you that he had never measured it?"

"Yeah, yeah he did, but I didn't believe him then. I figured any guy with that much dick has had to have measured it at some time! I'm sure he had, his tape measure was way too convenient!"

"So what did it measure when he measured it for you, or did you do the measuring?"

"Yeah, yeah I did. I gotta tell you that I wanted to handle that thing as much as I could, and so I told him I wanted to measure it. It was right at ten inches from the tip of it back to his body, and was like five and a half or six inches around, depending on what part you measured. I found one just like it, at the sex store, except it's white. Yeah, I use it on myself, but I just close my eyes and make believe it's black and him."

"You found one just like it, the same size, and you use that on yourself? Right?"

"Yeah, yeah. I mean that's okay isn't it? Gay guys do that don't they?"

"Oh yes they do, and yes it's okay! Only reason I'm commenting about that is, I assume – I assume, that does mean that that guy, that Thor guy, he did fuck your ass then, right? He did fuck you?"

"Yeah he did, but not until the last night. He wanted to earlier, fact is he wanted to the first night, but I wouldn't let him. I was too afraid to let him put all of that up in me. Tom, is your dick like his?"

"Uhhh, well not quite that big. Mine is more like maybe nine and five around. Mine kinda bends up in the middle. Did his bend any?"

"No not really, I guess not. You said yours bends up in the middle? How much? How big of a bend is it?"

"It's not a great big bend, but I will admit that for Bobby or any other guys to suck on it, it works best if his feet are up by my head so my dick will go down in his throat better. If he's got his feet down by my feet, it just don't go down in right?"

"Bobby, he's your partner, right?"

"Yeah he is. We've been together for about three years now. Great guy! You'll have to meet Bobby since you now know I'm gay. I just never kinda talked about me and my personal life at the company much, since I didn't really think it was much of anybody else's business, but now, remembering back, that day in the elevator, now that is a day when I should have said something. Remembering back on that day – really do think I could have at least gotten me some dick that day! So, hey – that dildo you bought, you use it on yourself often?"

"No not really. Well maybe once or twice a month. And yes, I will admit, that is always a night when you and I have worked pretty closely that day, and I went home horny as hell and had to do something. So I use it and make believe maybe it's you on the other end. But, you're never there!"

Once again looking around to make sure they are still in a private conversation, Tom asked, "So tell me about that Thor guy getting it up in your ass for the first time. What happened?"

"Oh that was my last night with him, and he was lying there on his back, it was looking like it was reaching for the ceiling light, and he put a bunch of Crisco on it, and told me to squat up on top of it, and to sit down nice and slow on it, and let it go up in me. I gotta admit, I sure as hell was not sure I should be doing that, but he kept telling me about all the other guys that had sat on it and that he had pounded it up into, and he finally convinced me that I could take it. I did, and I was damn glad I did! After I got it up in me, I must have bounced up and down on it for ten minutes before he had me lie down on the bed and he got up on top of me! I thought he was making mashed potatoes in my butt while he was doing me. Seriously, if I had ever heard of any guy getting it that rough back in his ass, there is no way I would have ever believed it! He pounded the hell out of me. I can't fuck myself with my dildo like he did. I wish I could, but I can't! Just don't work!"

"Uh, so have you ever been fucked by any other guy since then?"

"No, no. No I haven't, cause I guess I just never found some guy that I wanted to do it with. Like I've already said, it's gonna have to be a black man cause the white guys, they just don't turn me on."

Looking at Sid with a big grin on his face, Tom then asked, "You'd let me fuck you right? I could get up in there, right?"

Almost losing all control of his excitement, Sid looked at Tom and almost yelled, "Yes! Oh God yes! Oh shit, hell yes! Tom, don't ask that though and not mean it, don't do that to me! I've already told you how much I've looked at you and lusted over you, so please don't say something like that unless you mean it, okay?"

Leaning over toward Sid, Tom softly said, "I'm serious man, serious! I'd love to fuck that tight ass of yours! Hell yes I would! And I'm gonna before this week is over. Then you and I are gonna be going back to Philly and do a three way with Bobby. You will love letting that guy do you! Bobby is black. Don't know if you knew that or not, but yeah he is about my shade of black, but he is hung like a horse! Seriously man, I think a lot like your ole buddy Thor was! In for that? Wanna do that after we get back home?"

"Oh yeah man, hell yes! But Tom, do you think that you and I will get to do it together before we leave here?"

"Oh yeah man, yeah we will."

"But, how and when? Where we gonna do it at?"

Chapter Eight:
The Bathhouse

"Darrell, where in the hell have you been? I've been trying to find you all afternoon. Where you been?," Jay questioned Darrell as he came into the cabin and sat some packages down.

Rather looking around to see if it was just he and Darrell in the cabin, Darrell started to explain.

"After that deep heavy meeting about how to solve really volatile disputes within a company, I just needed to get out of here for a little while and decided to catch a cab into town and get some stuff to take home to the girls."

"So you've been shopping all of this time? You been shopping this long?"

Once again looking around to make sure it was just the two of them, Darrell continued, "No – not really. Jay – you remember that tall blonde guy from Detroit that was in our meeting Monday afternoon, and he talked about working in the auto industry?"

"Yeah, well yeah, I remember him, not too much about him, but yeah I remember him. Why?"

"He was downtown too. I was getting out of my cab on like, Fourth Street I think, and anyway, right as I was getting out, he came walking up right by the cab. Course he didn't know I was the guy getting out of the cab, and I didn't even know he was close by, until all of a sudden, he stopped and asked if I was Jay, from the Inter-Relationship Training meeting. Then I recognized him. He had another guy with him and after a little chit chat, found out the other guy was a local man, 'Skip,' and Todd, the Detroit guy, finally just opened up and told me that he hoped it did not offend me any, but they were headed for a gay bathhouse. He told me that he had met this Skip guy in a bar the night before and had kinda made these plans for the next afternoon, and since I was getting out of a cab kinda close by, he thought maybe I was headed there too. He said he decided he needed to just be up front and honest, of what he was doing, rather than to have us see each other at the bathhouse, after trying to act so straight and casual."

"Headed for a gay bathhouse? How interesting! I have to assume then that, that blonde guy – Todd – is gay? Right?"

"Well kinda! I mean, another one of those married guys that kinda does his thing, when out of town, and on the loose. He told me that he likes going to the bathhouses whenever possible, because of all of the action you can either see, or be involved in. Then he asked if I wanted to join them. Told me that it was now obviously no secret of what he was doing, and if I'd like to join them, I could, if I wanted to. I told him and that Skip guy about some of what has been happening back here at the cabin, and I said, 'Hell men! Since I'm doing things that I never thought I'd ever be doing, why not add to the fun. Yeah, I'm game. Might as well go home learning one hell of a lot more than just what they are talking about in those, rather boring sessions. And, besides if I understand some actions of some of the guys I supervise, maybe – just maybe, it'll help me understand them a little better, and make me a better supervisor. I can at least use that as an excuse, if I start wondering just why I'm doing this, right? Yeah, let's go, I'm with you.'"

"Skip looked at me and grinned, Todd did the same and we headed down the street only about a block and a half, and Skip said, 'Okay, here guys, here's 'The Gay Spot.' Obviously not trying to hide who we are, are we?'"

"Todd and I both grinned and Todd said, 'Well, let's just say that I'm glad I'm not in Detroit. The name is rather straight forward, ain't it?'"

"Skip grabbed the door handle, swung it open and we went in – into what was a rather dark room with what looked like a bank teller window. Skip obviously knew the guy behind the window since he said something like, 'Tony, special treats for these guys today. In town visitors for a meeting out at the shore, and so we need to treat 'em, real nice! Okay?'"

"Tony kinda looked up and said, 'Got ya man, got ya!'"

"I guess the treating us real nice was a clue to give us a big discount. The sign on the wall said, 'One day membership, $10.00 plus towel deposit of $2.00 - refundable. Locker, $10, Small Room $18.00, Large Room $25.00. All payments are for eight hours.'"

"All Todd and I had to pay was the $10 daily membership. Neither he nor I were charged any more. Skip – him I don't know about, cause he just signed like a 'check' that Tony handed him, kinda like signing at a restaurant. I really don't know just what the special fee arrangement was, but I guess Skip pulls some power punches around there as far as the cash flow goes."

"Then Skip kinda turned toward us and said, 'Hey guys, put your wallet, your watches and any other stuff that you wanna make sure is safe in these lock boxes, and he'll but 'em back there like safety deposit boxes.'"

"Then looking at Tony, Skip added, 'Not regular bath house visitors so, I'm kinda helping 'em find the way.'"

"Looking back at Skip, Tony simply said, 'Oh! Okay. Show 'em a good time in there okay?'"

"Skip told him, 'Yeah, will do guy! I plan on it!' I really don't think I really fully understood the true meaning of that comment, right then!"

"After all three of us placed our wallets and such in the lock boxes, Tony handed each or us a key for our locker and a towel. Skip waited to hear the buzzer on the door, and as he did, he turned the handle, and pulled the heavy metal door open."

"Stepping aside some, Skip then said, 'Enter gentlemen – enter.'"

"All three of us then went into this rather long looking hallway that, at first, did seem to be very dark. But after a few minutes our eyes, well anyway mine, did adjust to it, and it kinda was like they had turned on some more lights. Skip led us to the locker room, and we each looked for our assigned locker numbers, and eventually, did find 'em. We were all within the same general area, and only about an arms reach away from each other. We each opened our respective lockers, sat down on the bench and started the, rather required, disrobing. Obviously I was all eyes. Todd had already told me out on Fourth Street that whenever possible, he likes to go to gay bathhouses and of course Skip – from the money situation as we came in – was obviously a very normal regular, so I was the rather 'new man' to this type of an environment. So of course, I was keeping my eyes open. New kind of a place for me, and I was hoping for some new types of actions that I had never been involved in too much. Well, anything different than what had happened at the cabin in the last few days, anyway."

"Holly fucking shit man! Where in the hell did you get that thing man! Holly crap man, holly shit!" Todd was totally taken back when he looked over just as I dropped my briefs and my nine incher came bouncing out."

"Skip looked over to see what Todd was exclaiming about, but I was standing to where he couldn't see the front of me, so Skip grabbed my arm and turned me around so he could see my tool. The way Todd was looking and exclaiming, he just knew it had to be my rod that he was almost yelling about."

"Skip kinda let out with a, 'Holly shit, you are right man! Damn man, that is a beaut!' Then he added, 'Hell, if I had known out there on the street that you were hanging that much stuff in there, I'd have picked you up and hand carried you in here man! Darrell, you are hung like a fucking horse!'"

"Then looking up at me, Skip asked, "Did you tell us out there, that the only time you've ever done anything with a guy is here – this week? Is that right?'"

"Yeah, yeah. Hey guys, this kind of playing around is totally new to me. It all started kind of by accident, when I walked in on one of my group fucking the hell out of some coach guy, and from that point on, we've all been kinda doing stuff that none of us have done before."

"Then Todd quickly asked me, 'A coach guy? You say a coach?' "

"I told him, 'Yeah, a coach. He's here for the meetings too, but I gotta tell you I don't even know exactly where he's from. I kinda decided that since he's a university coach somewhere, and he's fucking his football players and they're fucking him back, I didn't think I oughta ask where he's from.'"

"Todd asked me, 'You know his name though?'"

"I told him – yeah, Stan. Told us, it's short for Stanley – why? You know him?"

"That's when he told me, 'Hell man, not as well as I plan on it! I know who he is. He's been in a couple of my meetings with me, and he is about as hot as hell as a guy can get! Big muscle man, right? He's fucking his football players and they're fucking him!? Oh shit man! Every time he talks, I sit there and undress him from top to bottom. I thought he looked at me kinda close like once, and I wish to hell now that I'd have, at least, nodded of something, to indicate, yeah, I play! I will be talking to that man before this week is up! I fucking know that! I'll find him some way!'"

As Todd and I were rather discussing one of Todd's future playmates, Skip stood up, grabbed his towel and said, "Hey guys. I'm headed for the steam room. Gonna join me?"

"Yeah! Yeah!" Of course, was the dual sounds coming from Todd and me."

"We closed our lockers and of course made sure the locks were all snapped closed good and tight, and Todd and I followed Skip down the hall, past a little sitting area, past the restrooms – well one restroom since the bathhouse does not need a lady's restroom, and then on into the steam room."

"We each hung our towels on hooks, on the outside of the room, and bare-assed as three guys can get, we pulled open the steam room door and went in. It was so full of steam that we really could not see anything! And when I said, 'could not see anything,' – I meant it! I did not even know how big of a room it was – did not know if it had benches or chairs or what, and of course I did not know who, or how many guys were already in there."

Then once again looking around to make sure nobody else had entered the cabin, Darrell continued with, "Jay, if you ever wanna see what getting grabbed by the dick and the balls by somebody that you cannot even really see, go to a gay bathhouse! Man – before I found a seat to sit down on, I must have had four guys either grabbing my dick or patting my ass."

"I later figured out the room was probably about twenty-five or thirty feet long, and about maybe ten to twelve feet wide. It had kinda like bleacher steps to go up on and sit on. Not bleachers, but rather built-in concrete 'big steps.' Men could sit up a step from another guy and be behind him. And let me tell you, the guy in front could then turn around and either grab your stick of meat, or maybe lean over and just start sucking on it!"

"Oh shit Darrell! Did somebody do that to you in there?" Jay emphatically asked, as he subconsciously reached down and rubbed his own crotch.

"Oh yes, oh yes! More than once. Jay, I do admit I've got a pretty good sized wiener on me, but I gotta tell you that, at no time in my life, have I ever had so many guys all wanting to do stuff to me, and all at the same time! I mean, yeah I gotta admit, that this was the first time that I had ever been in that kind of a situation, all bare and naked and hanging out, but I mean just in general, at no time have that many guys all wanted my attention like happened today. I mean even that Todd and that Skip guy."

"We got in that steam room, and just as soon as I sat down, Skip sat down right beside me, and I didn't even have a hard on yet, and he had his face down on my dick and sucking on me like some steam locomotive! And then Todd, he sat down on the step below me and he kept licking up and down my legs while Skip was sucking, and just as soon as Skip pulled off, Todd took over."

"I will admit it man, I had a major hard on like none other! I'm sitting there, Todd is in front of me, sucking on my dick like crazy, Skip is beside me and chewing on my tits, my arms, my neck and every other body part he can get to, and then there are these two other guys just trying to get in on the action, anyway then can. One of 'em took over for Todd after about probably ten or fifteen minutes, and that guy is the one that got a mouth full of cum. I kept trying to hold back on it, but with the way that guy sucked, he must have been come kind of a sucking champion, cause there was no way to hold back with him on my dick! He sucked like a major vacuum tube on some kind of a street sweeper or something. Jay, I kid you not, I thought that he was gonna suck my nuts right up and out of the end of my dick the way he sucked. I think he might have been maybe in his mid-twenties, so all I can say is, he sure as hell must have had one hell of a lot of experience, or one hell of a good teacher! I won't deny it, I wish he could go home with us! Damn man, he was one hell of a good sucker!"

"Oh shit man, God Darrell you are making me horny as hell right now, telling me that stuff!" Jay remarked, as he once again rubbed his crotch and now, also licked his lips.

"Holly crap Darrell, what in the hell happened then? What'd you do then?"

"Well, by that time, I really needed to get out of all of that steam. I had to get out of there and get some fresh air, so I headed for the shower. I thought I was the ring leader or something. Jay, I gotta tell you that I've never been in a situation where my dick was hanging out and a bunch of guys were all wanting some of it. While we were in the steam room, I heard some of the guys telling each other that, 'This guy is hung like a fucking horse,' and since it was so hard to see anything in all of that steam, five guys all followed me out of the steam room, and went into the shower room, and took a shower with me."

"Oh shit man, I can't believe this! I can't! So – tell me – tell me, what happened next?"

"Well we were in the gang shower, it had like about ten shower heads in that shower room, and there were two guys in there already taking a shower, and of course when we went in, one of 'em looked at me and said, 'Oh shit!' Of course then the other guy turned to look and see what the other guy was talking about, so then I had like seven guys, all trying to get close to it, but the guy that got lucky, if that's what you wanna call it, was the little black guy that was showering beside me."

"Little black guy? What do you mean, 'Little black guy?'"

"Well, of all of the guys in the shower room, Skip and Todd were not part of 'em, the little black guy was the one that kinda turned me on the most. He looked almost like he was too young to be in there, but I knew he had to be at least twenty-one or he could not have been in there, and he just plain-out told me he wanted me to come to his room and fuck him. I looked him over, he stood about maybe five foot seven, weighted in probably at about a hundred and fifty or a hundred and fifty-five, had the butt of heaven on him! Looked just like the halves of two big basketballs glued on him back there! And let me tell you, rock solid – rock solid ass muscles!"

"I guess what you are telling me is, yes you did go fuck him, right?"

"Yeah, yes I did. He reached over while I was still showering and all of a sudden, he was soaping down my back, and then down to my waist, then down my legs and then up and under my bag of nuts, and that was the clincher. When he put his hands up in there, it of course made my little swinger get a little bigger, and after he bent over and licked the side of it, then looked up at me and asked, 'You will fuck me, right?' I was taken. No way in hell and back was I gonna turn that guy down. He told me he was in room 102, down the hall and on the right, and he'd be there waiting on me."

"He sure as hell did not have to wait long! I rinsed off, removed a couple of hands that were trying their best to get me to change my mind of what I was gonna do, and I headed down the hall. Got to room 102, pushed open the door, stepped in, and found little Craig, as I found out later was his name, laying there totally bare, on his gut, with his ass all greased up and ready! He turned his head toward me, and just said, 'I trusted you'd be here. Close the door, and lay down on me.'"

"So I did! I threw my towel over onto the chair, laid down on him, and within one minute, I had my rod all the way up inside of him. I got it all lined up with his little hole, and I do emphasize the word 'little,' it was tight, damn tight, and man it felt good! I had already shot off once back in the steam room, but pushed up in that tight little hole that I was using on the back side of Craig, I did it again. I was pounding him and that ass like all from hell, and all of a sudden, he knew I was about to cum. He started yelling at me, 'Come on – come on –come on! Do it man, do it! Load me man, load me! Oh yeah oh yeah! Oh I can feel that – I can feel that! Oh yeah man, oh yeah that feels so fucking good up in there man, do it – do it –do it! Oh yeah do it again! Oh, I need that again, oh yeah, I need it again!"

"I flopped on his back, tried to take some deep breaths and tried to tell him that I was fucking exhausted and there was no way in hell that I was gonna be able to do it again. Oh man, what a tight little asshole that guy has got! After we both rather regained some breath and some sense of normal living and breathing, we talked a little and I did find out he was actually twenty-three, looked a lot younger, and was an artist, doing water colors pictures of the coast line. Haven't gotten to see any of his work yet, but sure would like to an maybe buy one as a gift to the wife, and secretly, a reminder to myself about the fucking he and I did together! Can you imagine having a painting, hanging on the living room wall, that every time I see it, it reminds me of the tight little ass on the little black guy, that I fucked the hell out of?"

"I don't know if I'd do that or not! Might kinda cause you some problems, every time you saw it. Probably give you a hard on, and then your wife would be wondering what was so sexy about that picture of just water and the coastline."

"Yeah, I think you might be right! Maybe I'd better not!"

"Hey, hey! Next step? What happened after the tight fuck? What happened?"

"Well, kinda maybe ashamed to admit it, but he talked me into sucking on his dick. Nice sized dick. Not as big as mine, but it was still probably a good seven inches hard, and it was fat and thick! Since he is a smaller kind of a guy, that dick looked pretty damn big on him. And yes, before you asked, I did take the whole thing. Chocked a lot doing it, but you know, my attitude right hen was, he let me use his ass for one hell of a good fucking, and yes, I know he liked it too, but I think I got the best of that deal, and so I needed to let him know I appreciated it. I told him I'd never sucked on some guy before. I really do think he turned out to be a pretty good teacher. Told me how to do it, and he was real patient with me until I finally got it all in. Jay, I will admit, sucking a dick ain't such a bad thing. Used to freak the hell out of me just thinking about some guy putting some other guy's dick in his mouth, but gotta admit, I don't think that's gonna be the only time I do that! Now I kinda know why guys do it! Not bad, really, it's not bad. Fun too! You know doing something like that – something real nasty and something that you have always been taught that nobody is supposed to do – hey – being nasty and trashy is kind of fun! Hey, it was fun! I'll never tell my wife I did it, but hey – it was fun."

"So after the dick sucking, then what did you do? You leave the bathhouse then?"

Once again glancing around to again make sure it was still just he and Jay, Darrell said, "No, I walked the halls for a few minutes, until that is, I was invited into some guy's room and asked if I wanted to get fucked. He told me that he really needed an ass to use, and he was hoping I'd let him fuck me. So I did! Nice guy, about maybe thirty-five or so, really tall, and kinda of on the skinny side, but a good fucker! Felt good! Probably fucked me for about maybe five minutes, then shot off and was done. So, I got up and left. My ass felt good, but I kinda felt like maybe we could have done something else, rather than just a – 'Slam, bang, thank you mam,' thing."

"So that's all he wanted to do? That all?"

"Yeah, I guess so. I saw him leaving just a few minutes after he fucked me, so I guess I must have satisfied him. Anyway, I ran into Skip in the hallway, and he asked me how things were going, and I had to admit to him that I was having a great time. Told him about me and the little Craig, and then the fast fuck with the other guy, and he said, 'Yeah, some of 'em are like that. Fast fuck, then home to the little lady and the kids.' Gotta admit, that comment sounded just a little too close to home, for me. But, gotta admit, I wasn't headed home after I got done there, so I just ignored it some. Skip then asked me if I would fuck him. He told me that after seeing my dick in the locker room, he'd been getting pretty anxious to take it up his butt hole. He said that if I would, he'd go get a room since neither one of us, and Todd included, had rented a room. I told him, 'Hell yes I'll fuck you! You look like you'd be a good butt to fuck." He was a really athletic looking guy. Probably about six foot three or four, tall guy, big fucking chest and arms on him, and legs of shear steel! He got the room, and after we got in there, I ate him up! I had never run my mouth up and down some guy, or even some gal, like I did him. His legs were a total turn on to me. They were sticks of steel and I mean it. Found out later he did a lot of running, and let me tell you, I need to start doing some running, if I can look like that! Hot as hell to just look at, so you can imagine what I did with him and those legs once we were in bed together, and naked."

"Oh shit man, you are getting me so fucking hot and turned on man, I never thought I'd be getting all hot and excited over listening about some other guy playing around with another man, but fuck – I'm about to explode! Come here – let's go in the bathroom where I can jack off and get rid of this cum. You stand by the door and if somebody comes in the front door, just close the bathroom door as if nothing is going on, OK?"

The two did move to the bathroom so that Jay could jerk himself off and shoot it into the toilet, and Darrell could shut the door if necessary. Nobody came home. The two continued their conversation, once Jay got all tidied up and flushed down the four shots of cum juice that he finally let fly, as he was listening to Darrell tell about kissing the romance out of Skip's muscled legs!

Darrell kinda shook his head, standing there, realizing that he was now standing at a bathroom door, watching one of his co-workers standing there, in front of a toilet, with his hard on in his hand, and as he listened to him telling about his adventures, his connections and the bodies at the bathhouse that afternoon, Jay was actually jacking-off! Shooting shots of cum into the toilet bowl. Even as a kid, he had never experienced watching anything like this with one of his buddies!

"I kid you not, I think I must have roamed up and down on those legs, kissing and hugging them for probably nine or ten minutes before I finally took some KY jelly that Skip had with him, smeared some on my dick, and some up in his ass, and oh man – what a feeling that ass was! Tight as a straight jacket wrapped around your chest! Man, that ass felt good! I kept running my fingers around up in there a hell of a lot longer than necessary to get that jelly smeared up in there! Damn man, fingering him was almost as much fun as poking my rod up in him! I'd love to be able to do him again. But, guess I'd have to re-schedule a vacation down here sometime, and then – if I've got the family with me, how in the hell could I get away long enough to go make love to those legs and that butt? I can just imagine me telling my wife that I gotta go to a bathhouse and fuck some hot hung muscled gay. Married life has its limits. Guess maybe I'll just have to dream about him at night, and just hope like hell I don't say stupid stuff in my sleep like, 'Oh Skip I love your legs man, yeah I do! I love your tight ass man, yeah I do! Oh Skip I wanna kiss your ass man, yeah, yeah, I do!'"

"So what happened then. You just fuck him and then get up and leave? What happened?"

"No, not exactly! I shot off in him, flopped down across him, tried to catch my breath some, and then all of a sudden, I realized that he had gotten out from under me, had gotten up on top of me, and without me hardly even knowing it, he had his dick up in me – as fucking far as it would go! I don't think it was an extra long dick, but let me tell you man, it felt like it was a fucking fire hose stuck up in there! Damn it felt good, and he sure as hell knew how to use it! And yes, when it shot off I thought I was getting it in the ass with a fire hose too! Damn man, I wish like hell, he and I could get together again sometime. What an ass to fuck and what a dick to get fucked by! Jay, I now love bathhouses – I do! I'm sure Philly has to have some up there, and I will tell you man, I'm gonna be checking 'em out to see if I can find me another Skip hanging around one of 'em. Damn man, he was hot meat – scolding hot meat! I was damn glad I went gift shopping for the kids! I was really the one that got the gift."

Chapter Nine:
Late Night at the Meeting

As Sid came into the cabin 'next door' to his own, he grabbed something to drink from the refrigerator, as Tom asked, "Hey Sid, did you have any trouble telling Bob and Jim that you were gonna be busy tonight and not be over at the other cabin?"

Sitting down with a big grin on his face, he looked at Tom, Jay, Darrell and Stan, and grinning about as broadly as he could, he stated, "No, not hardly."

All of the other four looked at him with question marks spread across their faces and Darrell then asked, "No, not hardly? Sid, you are saying that with a lot of humor in your voice and on your face. What's up man, what's up? Something to tell us maybe?"

"Well yeah, maybe. I kinda walked in on Jim at a rather inappropriate time. He was on the phone scheduling some "dates" for himself and Bob with a couple of hookers for the night."

Almost in union, all four of the others in the room, let out with a strong, "What!?"

"Yep! That's what I said! He and Bob are doing some women tonight, and I kinda came in all at the wrong time. I was not supposed to know anything about it, but I just kinda happened in right when he was negotiating the pay, and the actions that they were gonna be paying for. Both of 'em really freaked out when I came in, and I had to make a very firm promise that I would not say anything to anybody about what I knew. So guys, I never told you – OK? I just told 'em that what they do is up to them, and I'd keep my mouth shut, and since I'm kinda sure none of you guys are real anxious for them to find out just what we've been doing, we'll just keep our mouths shut, right?"

"Oh shit man." Jay said in rather an amusing manager. "So I guess maybe we're not the only guys here this week that are getting some extra activities outside of the schooling, are we? Sid, do you know if this is their first time or have they been doing this all week?"

"I really don't know for sure, but since I do know they have a cab picking 'em up at the lobby at about nine o'clock, and Wednesday night they went someplace in a cab too, I gotta assume that maybe tonight is not their first night visiting with the 'ladies of the night.' "

"Well I'll be damned!" Darrell firmly stated. "I guess our playing around is just doing kinda the same thing, but at least doing it with some new playmates that we'll be able to play with again later, after we get back to Philly tomorrow, and back to our normal lives. Well, that is except for ole Stan there. And Stan, we all gotta give you one great big 'Thank you," cause without you, none of this would have happened, and I think I can speak for all of us, saying that we are glad it all happened and that we've all got a new perspective on living. And I kinda think maybe Sid can be the most appreciative, since this whole experience has really given him a totally new direction in life! Right Sid?"

"Damn right man, damn right!" Sid eagerly stated as he lifted his glass in the air and proudly stated, "A toast to our man Stan, our man Stan! Stan, thank you for being the leader of this whole thing, cause without you getting to Darrell and getting some stuff started, there is no way everything for me could have worked out the way it did."

In unison, all of the men followed suit and saluted Stan with their glasses lifted high. And again almost in unison, they said, "Thanks man, thanks!"

"Okay guys," Darrell then stated, "we've got about an hour before our buddies next door leave to have their night on the town, and on their women, so we need to just kinda of sit around and do some talking so that we're not in the middle of our own private little sessions, in-case they happen over here for some reason, so let's decide what's gonna happen once we know they're gone."

"No problem for me to decide," Sid quickly said. "I know damn well Tom and I are gonna be using his room. We decided yesterday that he and I were gonna do it before we had to go back to Philly, and tonight is the last night before we gotta do that, so I already know what we're gonna be doing."

"That's not a problem for me," Jay stated firmly, cause I gotta use that telephone pole of Darrell's on me, and in me, at least one more time before we gotta do the go home stuff. I've been dreaming about getting that big thing up in me again all day long. When that speaker this afternoon asked us all to jot down some of the most important things that we had learned and will remember about this week, there is no way I can tell you how I wanted to write down in real big letters, Darrell's dick! But I was afraid that then he'd want us to pass the papers in, so I wrote some stupid thing that didn't make sense at all."

"Hey great," Jay chimed in, "but what about Stan here? He's the one that actually spearheaded this week for all of us, what about him?"

"Fear no more man, fear no more!" Darrell gladly stated. "In about fifteen minutes, there is gonna be a knock on the door, and low and behold, on the other side of that door will be no other than Todd, from Detroit."

Hearing that statement, all of a sudden Stan let out with a, "You're kidding! You're kidding! The guy that I kept telling you that I wanted to see if I could play with? The same guy that I couldn't find again? Darrell, are you kidding me? He's gonna be here!?"

"Stan my man, he's gonna be here. I knew how to get in touch with him, and since I knew how hot he was to play with you and that bunch of muscles you got all over you, and you had told me that you were trying to find him, I invited him over for the night. Guys, tonight's it! Tonight's the last chance we get, till we get back to Philly. Just as soon as Todd gets here, and we make sure the guys next door are gone for the night, that's when we really take advantage of all of our Inter-relationship training that we've learned this week, plus a whole lot more! And I think you will agree with me – the extra has definitely been the best part of it! Our company will never know what they did for this group of employees this week. Inter-relationship training my eye! All they needed to do was give us some nice quiet private time together and yeah – maybe a bed or two!"

ABOUT THE AUTHOR

Wade Wright

Wade Wright is a semi-retired father of two daughters and four grandchildren. Transplanted many years ago from the state of Ohio, to the Southwest, now living single – well with the exception of his Min Pin puppy, which has been his sole love for the past eight years!

Enjoyed two loving partnerships, both of which ended way before they were supposed to.

Wade Wright is also the author of *Yes, Cops Do It — Oh Yeah; The Two Straight Guys; Apartment 117; In Cemetery Park; Jay, Jake and Jimmy; The Carpet Installer, Totally Unexpected; Marshmallow Cream — and Hard Big Pieces of Chocolate;* and also *Family Matters: and sometimes, it just does not matter,* available from TheNazcaPlainsCorp. com, Amazon.com, or your local bookstore.

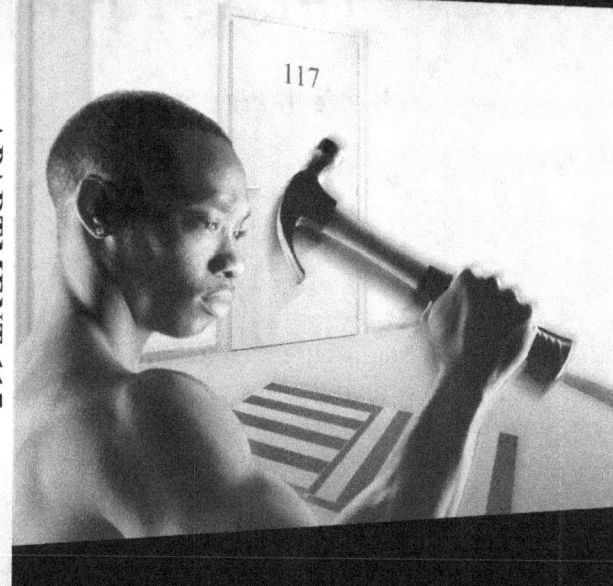

APARTMENT 117

117

a novel by

WADE WRIGHT

A BONER BOOK

FAMILY MATTERS
– and sometimes, it just does not matter

WRIGHT

FAMILY MATTERS

WADE
WRIGHT

A
BOXER
BOOK

IN CEMETERY PARK

A NOVEL BY
WADE WRIGHT

A BONER BOOK

JAY, JAKE AND JIMMY

A NOVEL BY
WADE WRIGHT

WRIGHT

JAY, JAKE AND JIMMY

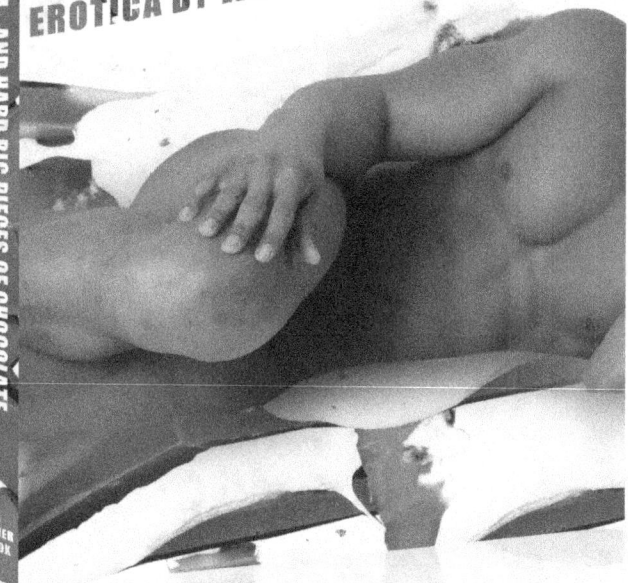

MARSHMALLOW CREAM
– AND HARD BIG PIECES OF CHOCOLATE

EROTICA BY WADE WRIGHT

The Carpet Installer

Installer

Wade Wright

A BONER BOOK

WRIGHT

THE CARPET INSTALLER

TOTALLY
UNEXPECTED!

TOTALLY UNEXPECTED!

A BONATI
BOOK

WADE
WRIGHT

"Yes, Cops Do It, – Oh Yeah!"

a collection of stories by

WADE WRIGHT

A BONER BOOK

The Two
Straight
Guys

a novel by

Wade Wright

A
BONER
BOOK

www.ingramcontent.com/pod-product-compliance
Lightning Source LLC
Chambersburg PA
CBHW051145260626
47170CB00005B/1967